Auntie's had an idea for the end-o

A Bollywood party sounded more inviting than a sponsored walk around the muddy playing fields. It sounded appealing. It sounded romantic. Hah!

'Maybe we can help, Auntie,' Geena suggested.

Auntie looked instantly suspicious. 'With the party you mean?'

'Or course with the party,' said Geena, wide-eyed. 'What did you *think* I meant?'

'That's very kind of you,' Auntie said. 'But' – she stared hard at us – 'there's to be no interfering. Do we understand each other, girls?'

www.narinderdhami.com

Also by Narinder Dhami:

BINDI BABES
BHANGRA BABES
SUPERSTAR BABES
SUNITA'S SECRET
DANI'S DIARY

bollywood babes

narinder dhami

CORGI YEARLING BOOKS

BOLLYWOOD BABES
A CORGI YEARLING BOOK 978 0 440 86513 1

Published in Great Britain by Corgi Yearling,
an imprint of Random House Children's Books
A Random House Group Company

First Corgi Yearling edition published 2004
This Corgi Yearling edition published 2008

1 3 5 7 9 10 8 6 4 2

The Random House Group Limited supports the Forest Stewardship
Council (FSC), the leading international forest certification organization.
All our titles that are printed on Greenpeace-approved FSC-certified paper
carry the FSC logo. Our paper procurement policy can be found at
www.rbooks.co.uk/environment.

Set in Palatino

Corgi Yearling Books are published by Random House Children's Books,
61–63 Uxbridge Road, London W5 5SA

www.kidsatrandomhouse.co.uk
www.rbooks.co.uk

Addresses for companies within The Random House Group Limited can
be found at: www.randomhouse.co.uk/offices.htm

THE RANDOM HOUSE GROUP Limited Reg. No. 954009

A CIP catalogue record for this book is available from the British Library.

Printed in the UK by CPI Bookmarque, Croydon CR0 4TD

For my Mum,
who loves Bollywood

CHAPTER 1

'What would you do if there was a hurricane right now, and the school started to crumble around our ears?' I asked Geena. 'Would you help Jazz limp out of the collapsing building, or would you leave her behind and make a run for it?'

'Oh, stop it,' Jazz moaned tragically. She hopped down the corridor towards the school office, clinging onto our arms. 'I am in serious pain.'

'I'd drop her like a hot potato and make a run for it,' Geena said without hesitation. 'Why should we all get killed? It would be so unnecessary.'

'I agree,' I said. 'Two out of three survivors is better than none.'

'Oh, be quiet.' Jazz winced in an exaggerated style. 'You're so heartless.' It was hard to be sure if she'd really hurt her ankle or not. She's a drama queen, and hypochondria is one of her specialities. 'I wish I was an only child.'

'Then you'd be even more of a spoilt brat than you already are,' I said. 'It's only Geena and I who are saving you from yourself. You should be thanking us.'

'All the research shows that it's the middle child who's the most badly behaved,' Geena remarked, 'and the oldest who's the most sensible and responsible.'

'The research is rubbish then,' I said with spirit. 'Mum used to say that I could be very sensible.'

'If you tried ever so hard,' said Geena.

'And there was a blue moon,' added Jazz.

Our mum died over a year ago. We didn't talk about her for a long time. We were trying to pretend that we were over it when we weren't. Our brilliant idea was to show everyone how over it we were by being totally perfect. You won't be surprised to hear that it didn't work.

We talk about Mum now sometimes. It's still hard. But when something hurts like the worst kind of pain you can imagine, you mustn't expect getting over it to be easy.

'I should be going into lunch now,' Geena complained. She stared wistfully at the clock on the wall as we passed at the pace of a snail. 'There'll be no French fries left by the time I get there. Really, Jazz, you're so inconsiderate.'

'Yes, if you hadn't been trying to flirt with two boys at once, you wouldn't have tripped over that football,' I added.

'My ankle might be broken,' Jazz said weakly. 'I'll have to go home. Do you think Auntie will come and collect me in the car?'

'You'd better not be faking it,' Geena broke in. 'You failed badly when you pretended you had flu to get out of that maths test last week.'

'Didn't Auntie want to put a thermometer up your bottom?' I said.

Geena and I laughed very hard, while Jazz looked like she'd swallowed several lemons.

'I've never seen anyone jump out of bed so quickly,' Geena chuckled.

'Let's face it,' I said, 'Auntie can't be fooled. Most of the time, at least.'

But that didn't mean we weren't going to try.

Since Auntie came from India to live with us a few months ago, she's been trying to look after us and Dad, but she couldn't just leave it at that. Meddling, interfering and sticking her nose into other people's business were the things she did best (or should I say *worst*). Anyway, it turned out that Mum had wanted her to look after us, so we couldn't really argue (well, no more than usual). Now we were trying to get along with her (sort of).

'It's a pity our idea to marry Auntie off and get rid of her didn't work,' I said with regret. 'It would all have been so *neat*.'

'*Our* idea!' Geena repeated sternly. 'I hope you

haven't forgotten exactly *whose* idea that was, Amber?'

'Because *we* haven't,' Jazz added, forgetting all about her so-called broken ankle as the opportunity to have a go at me arose.

'All right, so it was my idea,' I blustered. 'And it was a good one.' Geena and Jazz made mocking noises. 'But I admit it didn't quite work.'

'Quite?' Jazz snorted. 'It didn't work *at all*.'

My brilliant idea had been to get Auntie married off to my class teacher, Mr Arora. Mr Arora is the hero of Coppergate Comprehensive. His dark good looks send girls swooning in the corridors.

'Well, Amber' – Geena gave me a lofty glance – 'I hope you've realized that you can't go around sticking your nose into other people's love lives.'

'It would have been good though, wouldn't it,' Jazz said in a wistful voice, 'if Auntie had married Mr Arora? Every girl in the school would have been so-o jealous.'

'It might still happen,' I remarked. 'Especially now they've made up after that row they had at Inderjit's wedding.' Auntie and Mr Arora had met for the first time at our cousin's wedding reception, and argued (about us, naturally).

'And now Auntie's joined the PTA,' said Geena with satisfaction. 'She and Mr Arora had coffee together after the meeting last week, too. I heard Auntie telling Dad.'

'Really!' I said thoughtfully. 'That sounds rather promising.'

'But anyway,' Geena went on quickly, 'if we're not going to interfere any more, it doesn't matter one way or another. You and Jazz will just have to restrain yourselves.'

'Oh, of course,' I said sweetly. 'We can rely on you for information, anyway, as you're obviously keeping a close eye on them.'

Geena glared. 'I am *not* keeping an eye on them. I just happened to have noticed – casually, and without any effort at all – that they seem to be getting on rather well.'

'Is that why you were hanging around when Auntie was on the phone yesterday?' Jazz enquired.

Geena reddened. I grinned.

'Don't get your hopes up,' I said. 'She was talking to her friend Asha in Delhi.'

Geena and Jazz both looked disappointed.

'Oh, let's just leave Auntie and Mr Arora to get on with it, shall we?' I yawned. I was bored with the whole subject. 'If they like each other, they will. And if they don't, they won't.'

Geena and Jazz weren't even pretending to listen. They were talking amongst themselves.

'Did you hear *that*?' Geena whispered.

Jazz's eyes were popping out on stalks. 'Yes, I did.' She dug her nails into my arm so hard, I winced. 'It sounded like—'

'What are you two babbling about?' I began.

Immediately Jazz clapped her hand over my mouth, while Geena grabbed my arm and said, '*Sssshhh!*' loudly. She nodded towards the nearest classroom, 8A, my class.

I glanced across the corridor. The classroom door was ajar, but I couldn't see inside. However, I could hear voices and they were both familiar.

'That's Auntie.' I slapped Jazz's hand away. 'And Mr Arora!'

Of course, I headed straight towards the classroom.

'What are you doing, Amber?' Geena asked.

I paused mid tiptoe. 'What do you think? I want to know what they're talking about.'

'I thought we were just going to leave them to get on with it?' Jazz remarked.

'And then, of course, there's the whole question of sneaking around listening to other people's private conversations,' Geena said in a stern voice.

'I won't tell you what they're saying, if that makes you feel better,' I replied. 'I wonder if he's asking her to marry him.'

I was barely at the door before I felt Geena

breathing down my neck. Jazz wasn't far behind. Her recovery from a broken ankle in ten seconds was nothing short of a modern medical miracle.

'Well, that's settled then,' Mr Arora said. 'I know it will mean a lot of hard work.'

We still couldn't see them, but we could hear them much more clearly.

'Oh, I'll be glad to help in any way I can.' That was Auntie.

'And I'll look forward to working with you,' Mr Arora went on in his gently charming voice. 'I'm sure we'll make a great team.'

'If that's a proposal, it's the most unromantic one I've ever heard,' Jazz muttered.

'Ssh!' Geena and I whispered.

'Come in, girls,' said Auntie. 'Don't be shy.'

She has hearing like Superman. We all turned deep, dark red. Then we hung around for a few seconds, shoving each other. Eventually we shuffled in, Geena and Jazz sneakily hiding behind me because I'm the tallest.

'We weren't listening,' Jazz said immediately.

Auntie appeared faintly amused, while Mr Arora tried to look stern. They were certainly a very good-looking couple, sitting together at Mr Arora's desk. Auntie had lost weight since she'd come from India. She claimed it was the stress of looking after us. I'm sure she was joking. She was wearing a pair of black trousers, stiletto-heeled boots and a pink sweater, her hair knotted on top of her head. She looked almost pretty enough for Mr Arora, who was heart-throbbingly glamorous in a cinnamon-coloured shirt and geometric-patterned blue tie, black hair flopping over big brown eyes.

'You do know the rules, girls?' Mr Arora enquired gently. 'You're not allowed in school at lunch time unless it's an emergency.'

'Jazz has an emergency,' I said quickly.

'Doesn't she always?' Auntie said in a resigned tone.

'She's hurt her ankle,' Geena added.

We both stared hard at Jazz, who had roses in her cheeks and looked the picture of health.

'Oh yes,' Jazz said hurriedly, bending down to clutch her leg. 'Ow.'

'You didn't tell us you were visiting the school today, Auntie,' Geena said pointedly.

'I didn't know I was,' Auntie replied, a picture of baby-faced innocence. 'But Mr Arora rang earlier this morning and invited me.'

We all stared at Mr Arora with avid curiosity. He wilted visibly under our scrutiny like a week-old lettuce.

'I was just wondering if your aunt would be interested in helping us with our latest fundraising project,' he began.

It's not the done thing to groan loudly in front of teachers. I had to clamp my teeth firmly together. Geena did the same.

'*Fundraising?*' Jazz repeated in a despairing tone.

Things had become desperate ever since the upper school had moved across the road into a brand-new building, all glass, steel, space and light. The lower school (us) were still stuck in the old falling-down building, waiting for our part of the new school to be built. We were in for a long wait. A few weeks ago the school inspectors had visited us, and while Coppergate had had a good report, they were concerned at the amount of time it was taking for the new school to be finished. This had led to questions being asked.

The reason for the delay was rumoured to be that the school was running out of money. Tales of fabulous expenditure on the new building were flying all round the playground, with the head-teacher Mr Morgan named and shamed as the main culprit. All this massive overspending meant that suddenly we were being bullied into doing sponsored walks, silences and spelling bees by that tyrannical dictator Mr Grimwade, also known as head of the lower school.

'Yes, fundraising,' Mr Arora said sternly. The teachers had obviously been told to follow the party line, whatever their private thoughts on the subject, and whip us all into submission. He turned to Auntie. 'It's a very valuable lesson for the students to participate in paying for their school. It gives them a sense of responsibility.'

'Sir,' I began innocently enough, although I would never have been so cheeky a few months ago, in my perfect phase, 'is it true that Mr Morgan has a hand-woven carpet in his office with the school crest on it that cost five thousand pounds?'

'Someone said he makes everyone take their shoes off when they go in there,' Jazz added.

'That's nonsense,' Mr Arora spluttered. He caught Auntie's enquiring eye. 'It was just the once,' he said weakly. 'And they were Year Eight boys in muddy football boots.'

Geena vigorously joined the attack. 'And is it true that the staff room in the new building has got digital TV?'

'Yes, of course it is,' I replied. 'The teachers come in at weekends to watch it.'

'Girls.' Auntie stepped in to save Mr Arora, who was looking quite bitter. The staff room in our building hasn't even got a wash basin, never mind satellite TV. 'Shouldn't you be on your way? I'll see you at home later.'

'I think I'd better come with you now,' Jazz said in a weak-as-a-kitten voice. 'Seeing as I can't walk.'

Auntie ignored her. 'I'll give you a ring in a few

days' time when I've had a chance to come up with a few more definite ideas,' she said to Mr Arora.

We smirked and nudged each other. 'What ideas?' I asked.

'For an end-of-term party,' said Mr Arora. 'Your aunt's suggested a Bollywood theme. I think it could raise a lot of money.'

'It was just an idea,' Auntie said modestly.

I glanced at Geena and Jazz. We were all three quite impressed. A Bollywood party sounded more inviting than a sponsored walk round the muddy playing fields. It sounded appealing. It sounded romantic. Hah!

I could see it all. Romantic film music echoing softly round the school hall. Auntie and Mr Arora locked in each other's arms like Sharukh Khan and Manisha Koirala in *Dil Se* . . .

'What are you three looking so smug about?' asked Auntie as we went out, leaving Mr Arora with his packed lunch.

'Not a thing,' I said. I was secretly thinking that this romance wasn't dead yet. Oh no.

'How can I look smug when I'm in pain?' Jazz complained. 'Shall I fetch my coat?'

'Maybe we can help, Auntie,' Geena suggested.

Auntie instantly looked suspicious. 'With the party, you mean?'

'Of course with the party,' said Geena, wide-eyed. 'What did you *think* I meant?'

'That's very kind of you,' Auntie said. 'But' – she stared hard at us – 'there's to be no *interfering*. Do we understand each other, girls?'

'Oh, absolutely,' Geena agreed. Jazz and I nodded.

'Good. See you later.' Auntie went off, her stiletto heels tip-tapping down the corridor.

'But we *are* going to interfere, aren't we?' Jazz asked anxiously, as soon as she'd turned the corner.

'Of course not,' I said. 'We're *helping*. That's different.'

'Why should Auntie have all the fun?' Geena added.

'But we'll be clever about it this time,' I went on. 'I mean, it's not like we're *desperate* to get rid of her, like we were before.'

'We're just helping to smooth the path of true love,' Geena said lyrically. 'Pointing Cupid's arrow in the right direction. Oiling the wheels of romance.'

'And it'll be a bit of a laugh.' I grinned and nudged Geena as the two of us walked off down the corridor.

'Where are you going?' Jazz moaned. She limped theatrically after us. 'Now that Auntie's callously abandoned me, you've got to help me to the school office.'

'Try limping on the other side,' Geena advised her, 'if you want to be consistent.'

'A Bollywood party?' Kim looked at me over the top of her book. 'Sounds great.'

She carried on reading even though I was staring pointedly at her. Auntie had given Kim this book. It was called *Say No and Mean It!*, written by someone with the astonishing and unlikely name of Susquehannah Enkelman Gorze. Kim has assertiveness issues.

'Oh, for God's sake.' I tweaked the book out of her fingers. 'I'm trying to *talk* to you, Kim.'

'Is it urgent?' Kim asked assertively.

'Yes,' I said.

'Oh, sorry.' Luckily, after a few sharp words, Kim usually caves. 'You want to talk about the party?'

'No, about Auntie and Mr Arora.'

We were in the classroom, waiting for Mr Arora to arrive for afternoon registration. 'I think it could be on again,' I continued. 'Auntie's helping to organize the party.'

'Really?' Kim looked interested. 'But of course you and Geena and Jazz won't be interfering this time,' she added in an assertive tone.

'No, miss,' I said with heavy sarcasm.

'What's all this about a Bollywood party?' asked Chelsea Dixon. She was touching up her electric-blue nail varnish while Sharelle Alexander fed her Doritos.

'It's an end-of-term thing,' I said. I lowered my voice. 'You know – *fundraising*.'

'Fundraising!' Chelsea shrieked. 'Don't even mention that word.'

'My family hide when they see me coming home from school now,' Sharelle said mournfully. 'They put false names on my sponsorship forms and then they won't pay up.'

'What's all this about a Bollywood party?' George Botley shambled over to us, wearing his tie as a headband, his jumper lashed around his waist.

'My aunt and Mr Arora are organizing a Bollywood party for the end of term,' I said shortly. As far as I knew, George still fancied me. My aim, however, was to keep him as far away from me as possible.

'Bollywood? That's Indian films, isn't it?' George looked alarmed. 'I'm not wearing a turban. I'd look stupid.'

'Don't worry, George,' I said. 'You can be your usual stylish self.'

'Oh, great,' George said, relieved. The idiot then looked puzzled as Chelsea, Sharelle and Kim giggled.

'Sit down, please.' Mr Arora hurried into the classroom, the register tucked under his arm. 'George, kindly replace your clothes on the right bits of your anatomy.'

I glanced at Mr Arora. He looked all sort of pink and shining and glowy, as if he had a lovely secret. I smiled.

'Amber said I look stylish, sir,' George remarked, stumbling over his trailing shoelaces.

'I did not!' I protested. The rest of the class hooted with laughter. Even Mr Arora smiled. And, believe me, he does not find anything to do with George Botley funny at any time.

'He's in a good mood,' I murmured in Kim's ear, sliding into the seat next to her.

Kim grinned. 'That's because you said he looks stylish.'

'Not George,' I said, casting up my eyes. 'Mr Arora.'

'You said you and Geena and Jazz weren't going to interfere this time,' Kim reminded me anxiously.

'No.' I smiled. '*You* said that.'

'He's definitely interested,' I told Geena and Jazz later. We were on our way home after school, dawdling through the park, Geena and I dipping into a packet of M&Ms that I'd nicked out of Jazz's bag. 'George Botley was burping all through the register, and Mr Arora didn't even notice.'

'Absent-mindedness,' Geena said knowledgeably. 'One of the first signs of being in love. Do you want an M&M, Jazz?'

'After all, they are yours,' I said kindly.

'No, thanks.' Jazz smirked. 'And they're not mine actually. Someone left the open bag on my desk.'

'Urgh!' Geena spluttered, spitting hers out onto the grass.

I'd just swallowed mine and almost choked. 'Why didn't you say so?' I croaked crossly. 'They could have been poisoned.'

'Exactly.' Jazz began to laugh hysterically, so we set about her with our fists, which only made her laugh harder.

'Stop,' Geena said suddenly. We stopped just outside the park. 'Sorry, girls. It's Friday. You know what that means.' And she pointed across the road in the direction of the minimarket on the corner.

'Oh no,' I groaned. 'It's not that time again, is it?'

'Why do *we* have to come?' Jazz argued mutinously. 'Can't we just wait outside?'

'No.' Geena began herding us across the road like a determined sheepdog. 'It's less traumatic if there's three of us.'

I glanced through the window. Mr Attwal, the minimarket owner, was sitting at the till with his nose in a large book. He had possibly been the most boring man alive until a few weeks ago, constantly telling his customers all the things he might have done if only his life had been different. Then Auntie had come along and suggested that he do a few courses, take a few evening classes. Now Mr Attwal was like a man reborn. Or a bore reborn.

As we sidled into the shop, trying to remain inconspicuous, a bell louder than a police siren chimed overhead. Alerted to the presence of a captive audience, Mr Attwal jumped to his feet, beaming, and waved the book at us. It was called *Geography Is Fun!*

'Girls, did you know that Asia is the biggest continent in the world?' he boomed across the shop floor. 'And Mumbai is the biggest city – well, going by the number of people living inside the city boundaries; not including the people who live outside the city limits.' He was definitely the most boring man in the world now, for sure. His head seemed to be utterly stuffed with useless facts.

'Great,' I called out. I turned and elbowed Geena in the ribs. 'Hurry up,' I mouthed urgently.

Geena had it down to a fine art by now. As Jazz and I waited by the door, she skirted the fresh fruit and veg display, took a left by the tinned fruit and hurtled towards the magazines. Before Mr Attwal could step out from behind the counter and bear down on Jazz and me, Geena was at the till, clutching her magazine.

'Oh.' Mr Attwal looked disappointed. 'Is that all?'

'Yes, thank you.' Geena had the money in her hand, the exact amount. Five seconds later we were out of the door, breathing hard, Mr Attwal's voice floating wistfully after us. 'Come back when you've got a bit more time and I'll tell you all about the North Pole.'

'Do we *have* to do this every week?' Jazz asked crossly.

'Yes.' Geena unfolded her magazine. 'You know very well that Mr Attwal's is the only shop that sells it round here.'

Masala Express was only a local magazine, but it had become a kind of cult hit. I don't think it was because of the useful community information or the events listings or Auntie Palvinder's Traditional Punjabi Recipes. I think it was mostly because of all the scandalous gossip (not necessarily true) about local people. We thought we knew who they were most of the time, although no names were ever given. Now Jazz and I crowded round Geena as she flipped through the magazine to our favourite page, Geeta's Gossip.

'Look at this.' Geena read aloud. '"Who was the young newly-wed bride seen partying at Shannon's night-club with someone who was definitely not her husband?"'

'Ooh, that could be Baljeet Baines,' Jazz said excitedly. 'She's just had an arranged marriage. And her husband's supposed to be horrid.'

'I'm sure we're going to see Baby in here one day,' I remarked. Baby's our cousin. She's a good little girl at home with Auntie Rita and Uncle Dave, and a demon when she's let loose.

'Aren't *Masala Express* having a samosa-eating competition this month?' Jazz asked, trying to wrestle the magazine off Geena. 'Shall we go along and watch?'

Geena shook her head. 'Watching people stuffing down as many samosas as they can isn't my idea of fun. And the prize is only a couple of Bollywood DVDs. I doubt if it's worth the effort.'

'Next month's competition is a lot better.' Jazz pointed at the magazine. 'Look, a Touch the Car competition. Win a Ford Ka.'

'That does sound like fun,' Geena said with scorn. 'Standing there touching a car for hours on end.'

Jazz looked puzzled. 'It seems too easy.'

'Oh no,' said Geena. 'I've heard about this before. People have to stand there for ages, and they start feeling ill and hallucinating and fainting and stuff.'

'Oh, that sounds interesting,' Jazz said, looking more cheerful.

I wasn't listening. My eye had been caught by a headline on the opposite page: FORMER BOLLY-WOOD STAR MOLLY MAHAL – NOW A SAD RECLUSE LIVING IN READING.

Below the headline was a picture of a beautiful Indian woman in a typical Bollywood costume, a lilac and fuchsia-pink lengha with lots of body on show. She was dancing through a sumptuous *filmi* palace with fountains and golden statues of elephants. It appeared, shockingly, next to a photo of a run-down house with a battered green door. One of the windows had cardboard stuffed into the pane instead of glass.

'Look at this,' I said.

'Oh dear.' Geena pulled a face. 'What a comedown. From Bollywood to *Reading*.'

'Who is she?' Jazz poked her nose over my shoulder. 'I've never heard of her.'

'Molly Mahal,' I repeated. 'I think she was a star back in – oh, the early eighties.'

'That's ages ago,' Jazz sniffed. 'I wasn't even *born*.'

'Neither was I,' I said. 'But Dad's got some of her films. She didn't make that many, though.'

'Then she just disappeared,' Geena remembered. 'Wasn't there some sort of scandal?'

I was skimming through the article. 'Yes. She had an affair with one of her directors. He was married.'

'Really,' said Jazz. 'It's lucky that's not a problem in Hollywood. They'd have no actors or actresses at all.'

'Look.' I squinted at the photo of the house more closely. 'I swear that's Rosamund Road. You can just see the Indian sweetshop on the corner.'

Geena peered at the photo too. 'You mean the one Uncle Dave's taken us to a few times? It looks like it.'

'It says here that *Masala Express* tried to interview her,' I went on, 'but she didn't want to know.'

'Well,' Geena said, 'that's what recluses do. Reclude themselves.'

'How sad,' yawned Jazz. 'Do you think Auntie's making curry today?'

I didn't reply. My mind was off, winging its way down another track entirely. That was how I got my best ideas. Or my worst, some might say.

'I have an idea,' I announced.

The reaction I got didn't surprise me. Jazz stuck her fingers in her ears and began to hum. Geena stared at me in disgust.

'Really, Amber! I would have thought your

21

ideas had got us into enough trouble by now.'

'This won't get us into trouble,' I said. Oh, what famous last words. 'But if you're not interested . . .'

'Tell us.' Jazz took her fingers out of her ears. 'I could do with a laugh.'

'It would be rather good if we could get Molly Mahal to be guest of honour at the school's Bollywood party,' I said.

CHAPTER 2

Looking somewhat surprised, Jazz turned to Geena. 'Actually,' she began, 'That's not bad at all—'

'Don't get taken in,' Geena interrupted. 'That's how Amber operates. Her ideas *sound* reasonable at first. It's only later that the full horror really hits you.'

'You make me sound like Dr Evil,' I said. 'Anyway, Jazz thinks it's a good idea.'

'I said it wasn't bad,' Jazz backtracked cautiously. 'I didn't say it was good.'

'Of course it's good.' I spread out my arms. 'It's genius. Here we have a real Bollywood star—'

'Ex-Bollywood star,' Geena pointed out.

'Living just down the road from us,' I steamrollered on.

'About twenty miles away, actually,' said Geena.

'And we're having a Bollywood party at school. It's meant to be.'

Geena waved the magazine aggressively at me.

'Do you know what the word "recluse" actually means?' she demanded.

'Of course,' I said.

Geena ignored me. 'Molly Mahal wouldn't give *Masala Express* an interview. She obviously doesn't want any publicity. Is she going to turn up at our school party? I don't think so.'

'Auntie could persuade her,' Jazz said, her tone faintly bitter. 'She can persuade anyone to do anything.'

Geena frowned. 'That's true,' she admitted.

I was thinking hard, my mind zipping through all the pros and cons like lightning. 'No,' I said slowly. 'I don't think we should get Auntie involved just yet.'

'Excuse me?' Geena raised her eyebrows. 'I was starting to get ever so slightly interested in your foolish idea there, Amber. But without Auntie it's deader than a big fat dead duck.'

'Think about it,' I urged. 'If we can get Molly Mahal on board ourselves, we'll be in with Auntie like never before.' I grinned widely. 'We'll be heroines. She'll have to cut us some slack then and get off our backs.'

'I like it,' Jazz said instantly. Even Geena looked marginally more interested.

'All right,' she said grudgingly. 'It'd be worth it

to have Auntie at our mercy for once. But I still think it's doomed.'

I shrugged. 'OK, so it's a long shot. But Molly Mahal can only say no.'

'And she will,' Geena added.

'*If* she does,' I went on, 'it'll still be our idea, and we can get the credit. Then we can send in Auntie.'

'Deadlier than a cruise missile,' Jazz added.

We were wandering along our street deep in conversation and plans. So it took me a while to realize that someone was travelling alongside us, keeping pace. I eventually glanced up to see Leo astride his bike, travelling slowly along the kerb. Leo delivers our newspapers, and he and I have a love-hate relationship. Geena and Jazz prefer to put the emphasis on the love bit though.

'Oh. Hello.' I felt my face fill up with colour as Geena and Jazz started giggling loudly.

'Hi.' A fiery-cheeked Leo handed me Dad's evening paper, rolled up into a neat tube. 'How's your Auntie?'

'Fine,' I twittered, stepping backwards onto Geena and Jazz's toes simultaneously. 'How's your brother?'

'The same,' Leo replied. 'But the fund's getting bigger now. We might be able to take him to America for the operation this year.'

'That's great news,' I said, fiddling with the newspaper. 'Well. Bye then.'

'Bye.' Leo looked strangely reluctant to leave. He pedalled slowly away, looking over his shoulder, heading straight for a large pothole.

'Ouch,' Jazz chuckled as the bike lurched bone-shakingly into the hole, shooting Leo up into the air and down again.

'The path of true love never did run smooth,' Geena chortled.

'Shut up.' I waved the newspaper at them. 'I've got a weapon in my hand and I'm not afraid to use it.'

'What's that?' Jazz asked as something shiny and glossy slipped out of the middle of the paper.

I bent to retrieve it from the pavement. It was a copy of *Hip Chick*, 'a brand-new magazine for cool girls with funky style', according to the cover.

'He's made a mistake,' I said. 'This isn't ours. Leo!'

He didn't hear and was pedalling off. I chased after him. Because of Auntie, we'd discovered that Leo did two paper rounds, both morning and evening, helping to save money for Keith's operation to get his twisted back put right. Leo might get into trouble for delivering the wrong papers to the wrong house. I didn't want that.

I tripped and sprawled flat on the pavement,

narrowly missing a pile of dog dirt. 'Leo!' I picked myself up, ignoring my scraped knees. 'Leo!'

Leo skidded gracefully to a halt and looked round.

'This . . .' I panted, waving the magazine weakly, 'isn't . . . ours.'

Leo looked highly embarrassed. 'It's for you,' he muttered, and scorched away on wheels of fire.

Geena and Jazz strolled up behind me. '*Hip Chick* – "the magazine for cool girls with funky style",' Geena read out over my shoulder. 'The red-faced, snotty-nosed, grazed-knee look must be big then.'

'Maybe we should start interfering in Amber's love life,' Jazz remarked, 'and give Auntie and Mr Arora a break.'

'Yes,' Geena agreed. 'Between Leo and George Botley, she's got a more interesting love life than any Hollywood movie star.'

I took out a tissue. 'Hilarious,' I wheezed. Blushing wildly, which crimsoned my face even more, I stuffed the magazine into my bag. 'About tomorrow' – I reached out to stop Jazz opening our gate – 'we'd better decide what lies we're going to tell Auntie before we go in.'

'I think we should tell as few as possible,' Geena advised. 'I always find lies sound better if you stick to as much of the truth as you possibly can.'

'We'll ask her in front of Dad,' I decided. 'You

know how she's trying not to interfere so much.'

Dad had kind of left us alone after Mum died. But now, slowly, things were coming back together.

'Shall we tell them we're going to Reading?' asked Jazz.

'Yes,' I said thoughtfully. 'But not why.'

'Auntie will want to know,' Geena pointed out.

'All right.' I shrugged impatiently. 'We'll say we're meeting Baby.'

Uncle Dave, Auntie Rita and their kids, plus Biji (the most tactless grandmother in England) live halfway between us and Reading. They have a very posh house in the country.

'Oh, Auntie'll buy that,' Jazz broke in. 'Especially after you said last week that Baby was a bubble-headed bimbo who needed a good slap.'

'And what if she rings Auntie Rita to check?' added Geena.

'We'll have to risk it,' I said through gritted teeth. 'Why do you two always have to be so negative?'

'That's rather unfair,' Geena said coldly. As we trailed after each other towards the front door, I could hear her muttering, 'I knew this was a bad idea,' under her breath.

'Never mind,' Jazz consoled her. 'We can blame Amber when it all goes wrong.'

The exotic smell of garlic, ginger, cumin and sizzling onions floated down the hall towards us as Geena opened the front door. We all sniffed hard, drowning our senses in the rich, delicious scents.

'Want to bet Mrs Macey'll be here?' I said, kicking off my trainers heel to toe.

'Is the grass green?' said Geena.

'She'll be here,' muttered Jazz.

'Is that you, girls?' Auntie appeared in the kitchen doorway, wearing an I LOVE INDIA apron and holding a wooden spoon. 'Come and say hello to Gloria.'

We left a heap of trainers and bags behind us and wandered down to the kitchen. Our elderly next-door neighbour Mrs Macey sat perched on a stool, eyeing us over her cup of coffee like a frightened mouse.

'Hello,' she squeaked.

For months Mrs Macey had never said a word to us because she didn't like living next door to an Indian family. That was all before Auntie arrived, of course. Auntie doesn't stand for any nonsense like that. She'd soon forced Mrs Macey into coming round for coffee *and* being polite to us. Now Mrs Macey comes round of her own free will, especially when Auntie's cooking curry. She's discovered she loves curry. But she still seems a bit embarrassed about the way she treated us before.

'Did you have a good day, girls?' asked Auntie, stirring the curry.

'It was OK.' I turned to Mrs Macey. 'You should come to the Bollywood party at our school, Mrs Macey,' I went on, with wide-eyed innocence. 'Auntie's organizing it. With my teacher, Mr Arora. They're very good together, you know.'

Auntie reached for the potato peeler. 'Haven't you three got homework to do?' she asked, pointing it at my nose.

'Yes.' I ushered Geena and Jazz over to the door. 'An English essay on *Romeo and Juliet. Under love's heavy burden do I sink,* and all that.'

Auntie glared at me and stabbed the potato she was holding. Laughing noiselessly, I closed the door behind me.

'She'll get you for that,' Jazz predicted.

'I'll be waiting for her.' I caught at Geena, who was heading for the stairs. 'Where are you going?'

'Homework,' Geena began.

'Oh, never mind that,' I said impatiently. 'We've got other fish to fry.'

'I've never known what that means,' Jazz complained as I led the way into the living room.

'Just sit down.' I went over to the mahogany sideboard under the window and slid the glass doors open. There were heaps of videotapes and DVDs crammed inside. 'I'm sure Dad recorded one of Molly Mahal's films off B4U a few months ago.'

'Ooh, *Kuch Kuch Hota Hai*!' Jazz pounced on one of the DVDs as they spilled out of the cupboard. 'Let's watch this, we haven't seen it for ages.'

'No, this is it.' I had found a videotape labelled AMIR LADKA, GARIB LADKA – RICH BOY, POOR BOY (1982) in Dad's neat script.

'Nineteen eighty-two?' Jazz said, disgusted, as Geena switched the TV on. 'How old is this woman?'

Geena worked it out. 'She must be in her forties by now.'

Jazz looked dubious. 'Well, I hope she hasn't let herself go.'

'Let's see what she looked like back then,' I remarked, sliding the tape into the video machine.

The one thing everyone thinks they know about Bollywood films is that they're outrageous, melo-dramatic, over the top and unrealistic compared to Hollywood movies. So you think films about hobbits, boy wizards and flying superheroes are realistic? Bollywood films are just different. The heroes are usually good guys, the heroines are usually good girls, everyone loves their mums and the baddies get killed or arrested at the end, after various songs have been sung and dances danced. Things have changed a bit over the years though.

Now some of the films try to be a bit more hard-hitting and realistic, even if the hero and heroine still dance round a tree singing a love song.

However, *Amir Ladka, Garib Ladka* was still stuck firmly in the old Bollywood groove. It was about a rich, snobbish boy called Raju who doesn't really want to marry the rich, snobbish girl Tina (Molly Mahal) his parents have chosen for him. On his way to meet her for the first time, he gets mugged and, after a series of hilarious misunderstandings, which include losing his memory, ends up as Tina's family's servant. Nobody realizes who he is, but Raju and Tina fall in love.

'Remind me why Molly Mahal didn't make many films,' Jazz said. We were watching the happy couple singing and dancing their way through a lush garden filled with fountains and roses.

'She had an affair with a married man and kind of got blacklisted, I suppose,' I said.

'Oh.' Jazz stared intently at the screen. 'I thought it might have been because she's rubbish.'

Geena and I couldn't argue. Molly Mahal was very beautiful. She was slender and tall. Her hair was black and lustrous, rippling down to her waist, her eyes were wide, like cat's eyes, and toffee-coloured. She could dance. She could mime the playback songs beautifully. But she wasn't a great actress.

'Maybe comedy's just not her thing,' I remarked. We were watching a particularly excruciating 'comic' scene between Tina and the family's bossy cook, who didn't think she should be dating Raju. It ended with the cook chasing Raju round the kitchen with a frying pan while Tina screamed hysterically.

'No,' said Jazz. 'I think it's acting that's not her thing.'

We heard the front door open. Then a crash and a curse.

'Mind our trainers, Dad,' I called. 'We left them in front of the door.'

Seconds later Dad limped into the living room. 'You girls should put your things away when you get home,' he began sternly, then his eyes lit up. 'What's this? It's *Amir Ladka, Garib Ladka*, isn't it?'

We nodded unenthusiastically.

'Molly Mahal,' Dad said dreamily, sinking onto the sofa. 'She was my favourite actress when I was a teenager.'

'Why?' Jazz asked in disbelief.

'I think we can guess,' remarked Geena, as Molly shimmied onto the screen in a long, sparkling gold and green skirt with a thigh-high side-split and a tight choli which showcased her large bosom.

Dad blushed, took off his glasses and examined them closely.

'It's all right, Dad,' Jazz said kindly. 'We didn't think it was because she's a good actress.'

We watched as Molly Mahal began doing a dance number with lots of shaking around and jiggling of various bits.

Dad cleared his throat. 'Your mum didn't like her either. Said she couldn't act her way out of a paper bag.'

'Mum was absolutely right,' I said.

'Aren't you three supposed to be doing homework?' Auntie came into the room with Mrs Macey creeping along mouse-like behind her. 'Hello, Johnny.'

Mrs Macey nodded daringly at Dad. 'Hello,' she mumbled.

'Gloria's going to be joining us for dinner,' Auntie added.

'Surprise,' I whispered to the others.

'Oh, not this awful film!' groaned Auntie, her eyes flicking over to the TV. '*Amir Ladka, Garib Ladka*, isn't it? That Molly whatever her name is couldn't act to save her life.'

'Dad likes her,' the three of us said together.

'You know the rules, girls,' Dad said sternly. He reached for the remote control, and, with a supreme effort of will, turned the TV off just as Molly Mahal appeared in a denim miniskirt. 'No TV before homework's done.'

'Thanks, Dad,' Geena said with relief. 'I thought we were going to have to watch that utter rubbish for the next two and a half hours.'

'Why were you watching it, anyway?' Auntie wanted to know. She can never leave anything alone, she's far too sharp. 'I could have told you it was no good.'

'Jazz wanted to see it,' I said.

'Oh!' Jazz said indignantly – but had the wit to keep quiet after that.

'You can watch the rest later,' Dad said, picking up his newspaper.

'Don't threaten us, Dad,' I warned him. 'And by the way, is it all right if we go to Reading tomorrow?' I thought I might as well slip it in while he was off his guard.

'Reading?' Auntie was in there at the speed of light. 'What do you want to go there for?'

'I was asking *Dad*,' I said gently, knowing that she was desperately trying not to interfere so much.

Auntie struggled with her conscience and then bit down on her lip. I smiled triumphantly.

'Is that OK, Dad?' I asked. 'We're meeting Baby.'

Auntie snorted, a bit like a pressure cooker letting off steam. 'I thought you said Baby was a bubble-headed bimbo who needed a good slap.'

'She is,' I agreed. 'But that doesn't mean we can't go shopping together.'

Dad looked at me. I stared back at him with my best wide-eyed innocent stare.

'OK,' he said. 'That's fine, girls.'

Success!

'I'll drive you,' Auntie said suddenly.

'W-what?' I stuttered.

'I'll drop you off.' Auntie smiled helpfully, but there was a killer glint in her eyes. She was guessing we were up to something. 'Now that I've got a new car, I need some driving practice. Where are you meeting Baby?'

'McDonald's.' Weakly I said the first thing that came into my head. 'But we can get the train.'

Auntie shook her head. 'I wouldn't hear of it,' she said.

'That's settled then.' Dad opened his newspaper and started reading it, while Geena and Jazz pulled faces at me.

'Is it time for dinner yet?' Mrs Macey asked plaintively.

'McDonald's, you said.' Auntie took a right and headed into Reading town centre. 'I know where that is.'

'Yes, but Baby might not have arrived yet,' I said quickly. 'We're early.'

'Not a problem.' Auntie's eyes met mine in the driver's mirror. 'I can wait until she arrives.'

'Oh, you don't have to do that,' I said.

'I don't mind,' replied Auntie.

'No, really,' I said.

'But I want to.'

'Honestly, you don't have to.'

'I know. But I'm going to, and there's nothing you can do about it.'

We glared at each other challengingly.

Jazz dug her elbow into my ribs. 'She knows we're up to something,' she whispered. 'This was such a bad idea.'

I tried to think of ways we could get rid of Auntie. I knew that she was perfectly capable of hanging around for hours to show that we couldn't fool her one bit. But luckily, Fate took a hand.

We were winding our way slowly through the streets towards the town centre when Auntie almost steered the car into a bollard.

'There's Baby,' she said in tones of utter amazement.

It was almost too wonderful to be true. Our cousin was wiggling along the pavement about a metre or so away from us. The wiggle might have been due to her high stiletto heels, or because her stretch jeans clung like a second skin. A leather jacket was slung over her shoulders, and she was wearing a white top which dipped and plunged a little too much for ten o'clock on a Saturday morning.

Geena turned round in the front seat and grinned at Jazz and me. 'She must be on her way to McDonald's to meet us,' she said casually.

Auntie was still speechless. She tried to pull into the kerb, but she was so flustered she stalled the engine. There was a loud chorus of angry beeps from behind us.

'Oh, shut up!' Auntie muttered, shoving the car into first gear and bumping over onto the kerb.

I wound the window down just as Baby came alongside. 'Hello,' I said.

Baby almost jumped out of both her skins. 'Oh!' she gasped, sliding her leather jacket off her shoulder and clutching it to her exposed chest. 'H-h-hi.'

'Hello, *beti*.' Auntie turned to face me, looking sheepish. 'I'll see you three later,' she mumbled. 'Shall I come and pick you up?'

'No, we'll get the train,' I said sternly, daring her to disagree. She didn't.

Baby was looking puzzled. 'Are you going to see Mum?' she asked Auntie. 'Because she's not in. She's gone to the gurdwara.'

I scrambled out of the car as fast as I could. I couldn't trust Baby not to open her big mouth and give the game away. And even if she found out she was our alibi, I still didn't trust her. She'd enjoy making fools of us.

'No, Auntie's going home.' I stared hard at Baby. 'And *we're* going shopping.'

Baby stared at me in amazement. Then a sly, knowing smile spread across her pointy little face. 'Oh, I *get* it!'

'Bye, Auntie,' Geena and Jazz said, scrambling out of the car. We all surrounded Baby, silently daring her to say a word.

'See you later,' Auntie said. 'Mind you don't catch a cold, Poonam.' And she drove off.

Baby was smirking triumphantly in a way which made my hand itch to give her that good slap. She was going to get every bit of pleasure she could out of this situation.

'You told Auntie you were going shopping with me, didn't you?' she chortled. 'You owe me one, now. Boy, you *so* owe me.'

We looked depressed. Baby would never let us forget this. She'd twist the knife until it hurt.

'I bet you're going to meet *boys*,' she went on with glee.

'We're not, actually,' I said with dignity.

'We're not all boy mad,' Geena pointed out, tossing her hair around for the benefit of a good-looking guy loitering outside Gap.

'Anyway, why didn't Auntie Rita make you go

to the gurdwara with her?' Jazz asked suspiciously.

Baby suddenly didn't look quite so smug. 'I wanted to go shopping instead,' she blustered.

'On your own?' I said. Auntie Rita and Uncle Dave are just as strict as Auntie. Then it came to me. I grinned. 'You told her you were meeting us, didn't you?'

Baby looked shifty. 'Don't be stupid.'

Jazz, Geena and I started to laugh.

'So now we're even,' Geena said.

Red-faced, Baby flounced off down the street without even saying goodbye.

'That's sorted her out,' I said with satisfaction. 'Let's go. Geena, you must stop flinging your head around like that. You'll get whiplash.'

I had found and printed a street map of Reading off the Internet the evening before. The street where we thought Molly Mahal lived was just about walkable from the town centre. We set off, stopping every so often to check the street names.

'I think we're close by,' I said after twenty-five minutes. We had stopped outside the Star of India. 'I recognize this bit. Didn't Uncle Dave bring us to this restaurant a couple of times?'

'Round the next corner,' Geena said, studying the map. 'Then turn left and keep going.'

The streets were getting dirtier and more

depressing as we followed the map towards Rosamund Road. But strangely, the street names were becoming more and more exotic. We passed Jasmine Street, Carolina Street, Anastasia Close and Isabella Grove. Then we turned into Rosamund Road.

'This is it,' I said. I pulled the copy of *Masala Express* from my bag and studied the picture. 'There's the shop on the corner.'

Geena and Jazz looked around doubtfully. The street was crammed with terraced houses, the kind where you step off the street straight through the front door. Some had huge satellite dishes fixed to the walls. There was litter blowing up and down the gutters, and rusty old cars double-parked all the way down both pavements.

I stood there silently, thinking about the glamorous film star in the video last night. It seemed all wrong somehow.

'Maybe she doesn't live here at all,' Jazz said doubtfully. 'Maybe *Masala Express* got it wrong.'

'Only one way to find out.' I studied the picture in the magazine. The house we were looking for had a green door and an alleyway down the side.

It was easy to find. There was the house, looking even more dirty and battered than it did in the picture. The green door was scuffed and scratched

41

and the piece of cardboard which blocked the broken windowpane was still there. There was a tattered piece of paper taped to the peeling door frame which read, BELL OUT OF ORDER, PLEASE KNOCK.

'Go on, Amber,' said Geena. I could tell that she and Jazz were secretly feeling as uneasy as I was. 'Knock.'

Trying to look confident, I seized the letter-box cover and banged it hard. We waited.

'I can hear someone moving around inside,' Jazz whispered.

I pressed my face against the dirty frosted glass. I couldn't see anything except a shadow flitting about occasionally.

'I knew this was a mistake,' Geena muttered.

'Be quiet,' I said. I bent down, flipped up the letter-box lid and stared in.

I was looking into a dark, dingy, dirty hallway. Even with the restricted view I had, I could see that the carpet was stained and tattered and the furniture was the kind of stuff that no one wants to buy that you see in junk shops.

Then I jumped back, almost trapping my nose in the letter box. A woman carrying a suitcase had just rushed out of a room on the right. Without noticing me, she headed down the hall towards the kitchen. Next moment she was out of sight but

I could hear the jangling of keys, then the sound of a door being unlocked.

'She's running away!' I gasped.

'Who's running away?' Jazz demanded.

'Is it Molly Mahal?' asked Geena.

'I don't know,' I said, frustrated. 'But she had a suitcase with her.'

'That's a bit drastic, isn't it?' Jazz sniffed. 'We were only going to invite her to a party.'

'Quick.' I remembered the alley at the side of the house. 'We might be able to stop her, whoever she is.'

We made for the alley. It was quite narrow, so there was a lot of pushing and shoving which wasted a bit of time. Having the sharpest elbows, I got through first.

The alley went round the back of a garden that was thick with weeds. At the bottom was a rickety old fence, leaning drunkenly to one side. The woman I'd seen in the house was sitting astride it. She was leaning over, desperately trying to lift her suitcase up with her. This was so unexpected that the three of us stared open-mouthed.

Suddenly the woman caught sight of us. 'Who the hell are you?' she demanded.

I squinted at her. The sun was full in our faces and I still couldn't tell if it was Molly Mahal or not.

'Oh, hello,' I said politely. 'I'm Amber Dhillon, and these are my sisters Geena and—'

'I don't mean that,' the woman snapped. 'I mean *who* are you? Why are you here?'

'We're looking for Molly Mahal,' Geena said helpfully.

'Why?' the woman demanded in an incredibly rude voice. 'Do you want money?'

'No,' I said, puzzled.

'Well, if you're offering—' Jazz began.

'Shut up,' I said. I shaded my eyes with my hand and looked up at the woman. 'Do you want a hand to get down?'

She ignored me. With slow, painful movements, she unhooked herself from the swaying fence and slid to the ground. She landed heavily, falling sideways on one ankle, and, muttering to herself in Punjabi, stared accusingly at us as if we were to blame.

Then I saw it. It was just a glimpse, but it was there. Molly Mahal's face stared out at me for a minute, and then it was gone.

I gasped. I heard Geena's sharp intake of breath beside me. She'd seen it too. But the drawn, gaunt face of the woman, who was still staring angrily at us, the thin figure in the shapeless leggings and dirty fleece, bore hardly any resemblance to the glamorous beauty from the day before.

'We're looking for Molly Mahal, the Bollywood film star,' Jazz said helpfully. 'We thought she lived here.'

A fleeting look of pain crossed the woman's face. I suppose I should call her Molly from now on, although it was still impossible to believe. I tried to nudge Jazz subtly in the side. At the same moment, Geena stepped firmly on her toe.

'And what was that for?' Jazz grumbled.

'It's her,' Geena whispered.

'*Her?*' Jazz's jaw dropped several metres as she goggled at the slightly pathetic figure in front of us. 'Don't be silly.'

Molly Mahal's mouth twisted into a sardonic smile. Then suddenly, without warning, she closed her eyes and swayed slightly from side to side.

'She's going to faint!' I gasped. 'Quick, Geena!'

The two of us sprang forward and grabbed her arms. They were stick-thin, like dry, brittle twigs.

'Let's get her into the house,' Geena said urgently.

We helped her over the fence again. The back door stood open. We supported Molly across the weed-filled garden, Jazz trailing along behind us, carrying the suitcase.

'It can't be her,' she kept muttering. 'It can't be.'

The kitchen was a hell-hole. It was filthy and it smelled. The worktops were stained and caked with bits of food and there were electrical wires sticking out of the wall above the cooker. Gingerly Geena pulled out the only chair from under the tiny, cracked table and we sat Molly down on it. She immediately laid her head on her arms, and stayed there, very still. A gold bangle, the single piece of jewellery she was wearing, glinted on her right arm. It looked expensive, and very much out of place.

'Jazz, make a cup of tea,' I said.

Jazz was hovering just outside the back door. 'I'm not coming in there,' she hissed. 'I might catch something nasty.'

I went to the fridge. It was empty except for a packet of margarine, the cheapest you can buy, and even that was nearly gone. There were two used tea bags drying out on the windowsill, ready to be used a second time. Or maybe a third or fourth.

I raised my eyebrows at Geena, who looked grave. Then, quietly, I went round the kitchen opening all the cupboards. There was nothing in them except for a few more tea bags, half a packet of stale crackers and a pot of jam which was nearly empty.

'I suppose she wouldn't have needed much if she was going away,' Geena whispered, nodding at the suitcase.

'I'm not deaf,' Molly snapped, lifting her head

sharply. Her toffee-coloured eyes bored into mine. All the colour had bleached from her face and she looked white as bone.

'Sorry,' I said absently.

My eye had been caught by a crumpled letter lying on the worktop. I edged my way over to it as Molly put her head on her arms again. I couldn't see much because of the way the letter was folded. But a few sentences leaped out at me. *Eviction for non-payment of rent . . . Payment of arrears must be made within the next week . . .*

'You still haven't told me what you're doing here,' Molly said abruptly. She wouldn't have won any awards for charm. But I guess if I'd been a rich Bollywood star, and then ended up in a scummy house in Reading with wires sticking out of the wall, I wouldn't have been very charming either.

'Well, we were hoping—' I began. Then stopped. It was clear that Molly Mahal, in her current condition, was not going to be a big draw at the Bollywood party. It was also clear that I couldn't possibly tell her. It would be too cruel. I would have to find an excuse which would spare her feelings and allow us to leave as quickly as possible.

Except . . .

How could we leave, knowing that she was

probably suffering from having hardly anything to eat, and about to be homeless?

Geena always complains that I come up with ideas without thinking about them properly first. That's why my ideas are stupid (her words). Well, I did think about this one. But it was, very possibly, still stupid. I see that now.

'Well . . .' I began again.

CHAPTER 3

'This is a great day, Amber,' Geena said. 'It's got to rank as one of your best ideas yet. It's almost as good as when you persuaded Jazz that if you cut off her hair and sold it, you'd be millionaires.'

'I was only five at the time,' Jazz said in an aggrieved voice. 'I had a bald patch for months.'

'Yes, all right,' I said. I was already regretting my impulsive action. The train was lurching and rumbling its way back home, where I could only assume that even more abuse would await me. But what else could I have done?

'I had to do *something*,' I pleaded. I lowered my voice. 'We couldn't leave her *there*, could we?'

We glanced across the aisle. Molly Mahal was curled up next to the window on the seats opposite. Her eyes were closed, feet in cheap, worn trainers resting on her suitcase. Even though there was an empty seat next to Jazz, she wasn't sitting with us.

'What's Auntie going to say?' Geena demanded.

'We're about to arrive home with a woman who was a film star, and now appears to be a half-dead vagrant, and tell Auntie that we've invited her to stay?'

'*We!*' Jazz repeated. '*I* didn't have anything to do with it. I wasn't even in the room.'

'All for one and one for all,' I reminded her.

'That's such an over-rated concept,' Jazz retorted. 'It just means we all get to share the fallout.'

'There won't be any fallout,' I said, pretending confidence. 'Auntie likes helping people. She'll enjoy the challenge.'

'And it's quite a challenge,' Geena said smoothly. 'Miss Mahal wasn't exactly grateful when you invited her to stay, was she?'

'She was,' I said defensively. I hadn't mentioned the Bollywood party when I'd blurted out my invitation. I'd said that we were big fans of Molly's, and we'd be honoured if she'd come and stay with us.

Molly didn't seem to think there was anything odd about that, despite the fact that not even Geena had been born when she'd made her last film. She'd stared at me unsmilingly for a moment, then muttered, 'All right.'

'Either I'm going deaf,' Geena remarked, 'or she never even said thank you.'

'She didn't have to,' I said, trying to appear unconcerned. 'I could read it in her face.'

'And could you read her face when you told her we'd have to walk to the station because we didn't have the money for a cab?' Jazz enquired. 'I don't think it said *thank you* then.'

'Yes, all right,' I mumbled, flexing my aching fingers. I'd had to carry the suitcase all the way to the station.

'She could sell that gold bangle she's wearing to raise some money,' suggested Jazz. 'It looks quite expensive.'

'And what does she do when the money runs out?' I demanded. 'It looks like she's already sold almost everything she owns. Anyway, the bangle must be important to her if she's kept it.'

Silence for a moment.

'And where is she going to sleep?' Geena returned to the attack.

'I thought she could have Auntie's room,' I replied.

Geena's eyes flashed a warning. 'And what about Auntie?'

'I thought she could move in with you,' I said bravely.

'Then you must be mad,' Geena snapped. 'That is never going to happen, Amber.'

'Well, Auntie can't move in with me and Jazz, can she?' I pointed out in a reasonable voice.

'Thank God,' Jazz said with feeling.

'Forget it,' Geena retorted. 'But with any luck, Auntie will get rid of her as soon as we arrive.'

'How can you be so mean?' I said furiously, as the train rattled its way into our station. 'Look at her. She's got no money and nowhere to live. Why can't you try and have a bit of compassion for a change?'

Geena looked uncomfortable. 'Amber, *of course* I feel sorry for her,' she said at last. 'But she's not our responsibility. Her own family should be looking out for her.'

'I asked about her family,' I reminded Geena. 'She says she hasn't got any.'

Jazz sniffed. 'What if we invited everyone who was homeless to stay with us? We'd never get into the bathroom.'

'I'm not asking everyone,' I snapped. 'Just her.'

As the train shuddered to a halt, Molly's eyes fluttered open.

'We'll get a cab to your house,' she announced.

'I told you,' I began, 'we don't have enough money because we had to pay for your ticket.'

It was like talking to a brick wall. Molly ignored me, rose to her feet and walked off down the carriage, leaving her suitcase behind.

Geena smiled. 'Why don't you try and have a bit more compassion, Amber?'

I muttered rude words as she followed Molly off the train. 'Jazz, give me a hand with this suitcase, will you?'

Jazz ignored me too. 'We are so dead when we get home,' she said, walking away.

I sighed, dragging the suitcase towards the door. Geena and Jazz might be mad with me, but I knew they'd have done exactly the same thing. They wouldn't have left Molly Mahal there either. It was just more convenient to blame me. That way I got all the trouble that was going. I had a feeling there was going to be a lot of it.

By the time I'd heaved the suitcase out of the station, Molly Mahal was sitting in the back of a black cab at the taxi rank. She had a stern, implacable look on her face. Geena and Jazz, meanwhile, were hovering helplessly by the open door.

'She won't get out,' Jazz wailed.

'Look, love,' the taxi driver said patiently, 'do you want this cab or not?'

'Yes, we do,' I said.

'This is getting better,' Geena groaned, as the driver hopped out and stowed the suitcase in the boot. 'We roll up with the guest from hell, and get Auntie to pay for it. Oh, I can't wait.'

'What if they're not in?' asked Jazz.

'We'll rob the jar of change that Dad hides under his bed,' I said, giving her a push. 'Just get in the car.'

The journey was made in silence. Molly Mahal stared out of the window, her face a complete blank. I had no clue what she was thinking or feeling. Geena looked worried and Jazz petrified. Meanwhile, I was trying to decide how to break the news to Auntie that we had a house guest. There seemed no other option but to tell the truth, terrifying as it sounded.

My heart lurched horribly as we pulled into our street.

'I have to go inside and get the money from my aunt,' I told the driver as he drew to a halt outside our house.

He looked a bit suspicious. 'All right, but your mum and your sisters can wait here till you come back.'

'I'm not their mother,' Molly Mahal snapped.

'There is a god,' Geena muttered.

'Just wait here,' I said. The way things were going, they'd be at each other's throats before I got back with the £4.65.

I scrambled out. I was only halfway up the path when the front door was flung open and Auntie dashed out, looking concerned.

'Why are you in a taxi?' she demanded. 'Has someone been hurt?'

'No, of course not,' I said. 'But we need four pounds sixty-five for the fare.'

Auntie peered down the garden. 'Who's the old woman?' she wanted to know.

I took a breath. 'All right, this is the short version,' I said. 'We saw in *Masala Express* that Molly Mahal was living in Reading so we decided to invite her to the Bollywood party. It was a surprise for you. But she's got no money, so we brought her home to stay with us for a bit.'

'Nice try, Amber.' Auntie fixed me with a piercing stare. 'Now, the truth, if you please.'

'That's it,' I said. 'Look.' I tugged the copy of *Masala Express* out of my bag and handed it to her. Auntie glanced at the article and then back at the taxi.

'*That's* Molly Mahal?' she asked incredulously.

'I'm afraid so,' I replied.

At that moment Molly Mahal rapped on the cab window and waved her hand imperiously at me. Auntie stared at her in amazement.

'Can we have the money?' I asked with urgency.

Auntie nodded as if in a trance, went inside and came back with her purse. She took out a five-pound note and handed it to me. I'd never seen her so utterly lost for words.

'Wait a minute,' Auntie said suddenly as I turned away, clutching the money. 'What do you mean, you've brought her to stay for a bit?'

'She was about to be evicted,' I explained. 'We couldn't leave her there, could we?'

I scooted off down the path while Auntie stared after me, her mouth open. She watched in disbelief as I paid the driver, and Molly Mahal climbed out of the cab. Geena hauled the suitcase out, cursing under her breath.

'My aunt's really pleased that you're coming to stay,' I told Molly, who inclined her head in a stately manner.

'She looks it,' Jazz muttered.

Auntie blinked hard as Molly shuffled up the path towards her. Those trainers, those leggings, that fleece did not add up to a superstar. But Molly Mahal didn't seem one bit embarrassed. Or maybe she was totally embarrassed and was covering it up very well. She was an actress, after all, even if she wasn't very good at it.

'Er – *saat siri akaal*,' Auntie stammered, putting her palms together.

Molly Mahal returned the greeting. Then she stood waiting by the front door, her face still an unemotional mask. I stood next to her, wondering what Auntie would do. Geena and Jazz lurked behind us, trying not to catch Auntie's eye. Mrs

Macey, meanwhile, was goggling at us from behind her net curtains.

'Please come in,' Auntie said faintly.

Molly Mahal walked into the house without a word. We all proceeded solemnly into the living room, where she sat on the sofa and stared down at her hands in silence.

'Tea,' said Auntie desperately. 'I'll make some tea. And maybe you three girls would like to help me.' It was a threat, not a request.

'I'll stay here and keep Miss Mahal company,' I said quickly.

'Kitchen. Now,' said Auntie, and went out.

'Leave all the talking to me,' I said in an under-tone to Geena and Jazz as we followed her.

'Oh, OK,' said Geena. 'Another great idea.'

'Look, if we stick together, it'll be fine,' I said.

We shuffled guiltily into the kitchen and Auntie snapped the door shut behind us.

'It's all Amber's fault,' Jazz said.

'Thank you,' I muttered.

Auntie put her hands on her hips. 'What on earth has got into you, Amber?' she demanded, her eyes flashing sparks. 'She can't stay here. We don't have the space, for a start.'

'I thought she could have your room,' I said.

'And I sleep where?'

'Well, Geena's got a double bed.'

Geena and Auntie stared at each other ferociously.

'That's not going to happen,' Auntie snapped. 'Look, she must have some family. Or what about Social Services? There must be somewhere she can go.'

'There is,' I said dramatically. 'The streets. If we turn her away, she'll be homeless.' I opened the fridge. 'Can we give her something to eat? She almost fainted before. I don't think she's been eating properly.'

For the first time Auntie looked uncertain. 'What do you mean?'

'There was hardly any food in the place,' I explained.

Auntie opened the biscuit jar and shook some chocolate digestives onto a plate. 'There are samosas in the fridge,' she said. She frowned. I could see that I'd given her something to think about.

'Thank you,' I said.

I carried the plates into the living room. Molly Mahal still sat on the sofa, in the same position.

'Where are your parents?' she asked abruptly.

'Dad's gone to his office to pick up some work.' I took a breath for the bit I always hated explaining. 'Mum's dead. She had leukaemia. Auntie looks after us now.'

Molly's eyes grew dark. I had the faintest feeling she was going to say something more. But she didn't. She simply nodded a thank-you at me as I put the plates down on the coffee table and withdrew. But I got the feeling that she was only holding herself back by the greatest effort of will, and that once I'd closed the door behind me, she'd fall on the food like a wild animal.

'Amber, are you absolutely sure she has no family close by?' Auntie asked as I returned to the kitchen.

'She said not,' I replied. I switched the kettle on. 'She hasn't got anybody. Not in England, anyway.'

'Maybe she's fallen out with them,' Geena suggested. 'She's not exactly Miss Congeniality.'

'Neither would you be, in those circumstances,' Auntie replied.

'See?' I looked triumphantly at Geena and Jazz. I had secretly been regretting what I'd done since – oh – about thirty seconds after I'd invited Molly to stay. But I wouldn't admit it. 'Auntie understands. I knew she would.'

'You're not off the hook yet, miss.' Auntie threw me a warning glance. 'There are still several issues to be dealt with here. Like why you lied and told me you were going shopping with Baby, for example.'

'Oh, *that*—' I began. Luckily, right then we heard the front door open.

'It's Dad,' said Geena.

'Stop him,' I said, 'before he goes into the living room and gets the shock of his life.'

Jazz opened the door and we charged down the hall, Auntie included. Dad was in the process of taking off his leather jacket. He paused, one sleeve on and one sleeve off, a look of bewilderment on his face.

'What's the matter?' he asked.

'Quick,' I said, grabbing one arm. 'In here.'

Auntie grabbed the other, and we hustled him into the kitchen.

'What in heaven's name is going on?' Dad asked. 'Is the taxman here?'

'Worse,' said Jazz. 'We found Molly Mahal living in Reading, and Amber said we had to bring her home with us because she was poor and had no food.'

'Well, I felt sorry for her,' I said defensively.

Dad looked at us as if our brains had dangerously overheated.

'And she's hideous,' Jazz added.

'She's kind of dull and grey and very skinny,' Geena went on.

'Oh, my God.' Dad clutched his hair, looking horrified. 'I've read about this. They say soft drugs are everywhere these days. That people are even selling them at the school gates—'

'Oh, for heaven's sake, Johnny,' Auntie said, looking exasperated. 'We're not hallucinating. She's in our front room right now, eating samosas.'

'Not you too?' Dad moaned.

'Read this.' I pulled the battered copy of *Masala Express* from the back pocket of my jeans and handed it to him. Dad skimmed through it, shooting us nervous glances every so often.

'So you went to find her?' Dad was still looking puzzled. 'Why?'

'For the Bollywood party at school,' I explained. 'We wanted to help Auntie organize it.'

'I'm sure you didn't have any ulterior motives at all,' Auntie said smoothly.

'Absolutely not,' I said with a dignity that was spoiled by Jazz and Geena sniggering. 'We thought Molly Mahal could be the guest of honour.'

'Except that she's more likely to send people running and screaming from the hall,' Jazz said helpfully.

Dad was looking unnerved. 'She can't have changed that much,' he said. 'How old is she? Early forties?'

'She looks more like sixty,' Jazz said.

'And that's probably a conservative estimate,' added Geena.

Dad looked stunned. 'How long is she staying?'

Strangely, that was one question everyone, including me, had failed to ask.

'Oh, only for a bit,' I replied as casually as I could.

Auntie pounced. 'You mean you haven't discussed it with her?'

'Er. Um.' I tried to think of a lie. Couldn't. 'No.'

Dad and Auntie stared at each other, concern etched on their faces. 'Is she going to look for a job then?' Auntie wanted to know. 'Or is she expecting money from relatives?'

'I don't know,' I mumbled, beginning to sweat. I was saved by the sound of the living-room door opening.

'That's her!' Geena hissed. 'She's coming out.'

Dad opened the kitchen door and we all hovered in the entrance like people at a zoo queuing to see a rare animal.

Molly Mahal came out of the living room. She stopped when she saw us. A wary look flashed across her face before the mask came down again.

Dad seemed transfixed by her ravaged beauty. He stared at her until Auntie elbowed him hard in the ribs.

'*Saat siri akaal*,' he spluttered. 'I'm very pleased to meet you.'

'This is my dad,' I said.

Molly managed a faint smile. 'Good afternoon,' she said with surprising dignity. 'May I go to my room now?'

'It's the one next to the bathroom,' I said quickly.

There was a protesting noise from Auntie, which she quickly choked back. Taking no further notice of us, Molly went up the stairs. A moment later we heard Auntie's bedroom door close.

'Well!' Auntie said grumpily. 'She's a cool customer.'

Geena and Jazz grinned at me. It wasn't often we saw Auntie at a complete loss.

'I would never have believed it.' Dad tottered into the living room and sank down onto the sofa. 'I'd never have recognized her.' He shook his head in disbelief.

'She must have been starving.' Geena stared down at the plates. There had been six samosas, and they were gone. So were the chocolate biscuits.

I glanced sideways at Geena. She looked as if she was regretting some of the things she'd said.

'Talking of starvation,' Jazz grumbled, 'when's lunch?'

'Not yet,' Auntie snapped. 'We'd better wait for our guest to come downstairs.'

We all glanced upwards as we heard the bedroom door open, then footsteps overhead. There was the sound of water flooding into the bath.

'I'll just pop upstairs and move some of my stuff while she's in the bathroom,' Auntie said.

'Where to?' Geena asked freezingly.

'Well, your room, of course,' Auntie replied. 'Unless you want me to sleep in the shed?'

'There *is* a paraffin heater out there, you know,' Geena began.

Auntie glared at her and whisked out of the room. Seconds later she was back, looking aggrieved. 'Can you believe this?' she gasped. 'She's only gone and locked the bedroom door.'

'I told you it wasn't a good idea to put that lock on there,' Jazz said smugly.

'It was to stop you helping yourself to my Chanel cosmetics,' Auntie snapped. She began pacing up and down like a caged animal. 'I'm getting a bad feeling about this.'

'Don't worry, Auntie,' I said cheerfully. 'That's exactly how we felt when *you* arrived.'

'And look how well that's turned out,' Geena said with a straight face.

'Don't be cheeky, girls,' Dad said sternly.

'Sorry,' we both muttered.

Auntie was standing by the open door, sniffing the air like a tracker dog. 'That's my Chanel Number Five bath oil,' she groaned. 'Oh no! Twenty-five pounds a bottle.'

'She must be using loads of it as well,' Geena said helpfully, 'if we can smell it down here.'

We sat and waited. Half an hour went by. We heard the bathroom door open again. An hour passed.

'What *is* she doing up there?' Auntie wanted to know.

'Ssh!' I'd heard the creak of the bedroom door. 'She's coming!'

'Look casual,' Dad instructed us. 'Don't look like we've been waiting for her.'

'Like this?' Jazz flung herself down on the sofa, clutching her stomach. 'Help. I'm dying of mal-nutrition.'

We waited in silence, listening to each light foot-step coming closer. The living-room door opened.

Molly Mahal stood in the doorway. The effect, compared to her previous incarnation, was – well, dazzling. That's the word.

She sparkled. She was dressed in a lilac-coloured skirt and top, stitched with gold swirls and heavy with sequins. She didn't look stick-thin any more, but slender and wand-like. Miraculously, her bosoms had reappeared. Gold earrings with purple stones were in her ears and a slim gold chain around her neck. As she moved into the room, gold bangles jangled musically on both her wrists. She smelled deliciously of Chanel Number 5. Her make-up was skilfully applied, and while it couldn't disguise the fact that she was old, she looked a hundred times better than before. The effect was that of a snake shedding its dull, grey, outer skin and emerging newly dressed in brilliant, jewelled colours.

We couldn't help staring. She looked like a different person. She moved like a different person. Regal and queen-like, she swayed confidently across the room, and sat down on the sofa, arranging her silky, sequinned skirt around her feet.

Auntie looked more stunned than any of us. 'That's one of my suits,' she began in a dazed voice.

'And I'm very grateful to you for letting me borrow it,' Molly said graciously. Suddenly, her whole personality seemed to have changed. It was as if *she* was doing *us* a favour by being here, rather than the other way round. 'Thank you *so* much. I do appreciate it.'

Auntie was speechless. I looked down to hide a smile. What could Auntie say now without looking mean and nasty? Molly Mahal was *smart*.

Molly glanced around the room, her gaze coming to rest on the video recorder and the tape which had been ejected but not removed. '*Amir Ladka, Garib Ladka*,' she said in a thrilled voice. 'A wonderful film.'

'She's only saying that because she's in it,' Jazz muttered.

'Shall we watch it now?' Molly went on, fluttering her eyelashes at Dad. It was more of a command than a request.

Geena and I looked at each other, aghast. We'd already sat through forty terrible minutes of it. I couldn't imagine that it would get any better on a second showing.

'What about lunch?' Jazz wailed.

'Oh, surely we have time to watch just a little before we eat?' Molly enquired in a sweet but steely voice.

'Certainly,' said Dad politely. He'd already slotted the videotape into the machine. Gloomily we sat back and prepared for a second showing of probably one of the worst films ever to come out of Bollywood.

Molly beamed as the credits began. She then swung round to stare accusingly at me as I wiggled into a more comfortable position on the sofa, the leather cushion squeaking ever so slightly.

'Do you think we're allowed to breathe?' Geena whispered in my ear.

The film began. To our dismay, Molly took charge of the remote control, and whenever there was a part she thought was particularly good, she re-ran the tape and watched it again. This made the film seem twice as long. Predictably, the bits she thought were good were only ever the bits that she was in.

When we got to the scene with the mad cook and the frying pan, Jazz could stand it no longer. She got quietly to her feet and sidled out of the room.

Molly Mahal sent a laser-beam stare after her. 'We're just coming to a very exciting part,' she remarked coolly. 'I hope she won't be long.'

'Just as long as it takes to eat her way through the entire contents of the fridge,' I whispered to Geena, which earned me another look.

Jazz wasn't very long, however. She reappeared a few minutes later and edged her way back into the room, casting nervous glances at Molly Mahal.

'Auntie,' she mouthed.

'What?' Auntie mouthed back.

Molly shot them both a 'this had better be important' look.

'I've set the grill on fire,' Jazz whispered.

'What!' Auntie shrieked. She leaped to her feet and dashed out of the room.

'Well, really!' Molly Mahal looked mightily annoyed. 'Some of us are trying to watch a good film in peace.'

Geena and I took the opportunity to leave the room as quietly as we could, too. Jazz trailed along behind us, muttering to herself.

Auntie was beating out the flames in the grill pan with a wet towel. Luckily there didn't seem to be any damage done.

'I was trying to make cheese on toast,' Jazz said dismally.

'Well done.' I slapped her on the back. 'You saved us from having to watch the rest of *Amir Ladka, Garib Ladka*.'

Auntie was banging round the kitchen, wiping out the grill pan and muttering to herself. 'I don't know why the woman needs to borrow my best clothes to sit around the house and watch herself in a movie,' she complained. 'She's even borrowed my underwear.'

'Ooh, how do you know?' Jazz asked. 'Did you look?'

Auntie gave her a withering stare. 'She had no chest when she arrived, and now she has. She must be wearing my Wonderbra.'

'I didn't know you had a Wonderbra,' I said with interest.

'I don't discuss the contents of my underwear drawer with you,' Auntie said coldly.

Dad came into the kitchen. 'Miss Mahal says we'll watch the rest of the film after lunch,' he said. 'I've stopped the tape.'

'Dad,' I groaned. 'Do we have to?'

'Yes, we do.' Dad looked stern. 'She's our guest.'

'Happy now, Amber?' Geena enquired with savage politeness. Jazz contented herself with an eloquent sniff.

'And she'd prefer curry for lunch,' Dad added. 'If it's no trouble.'

Auntie stopped mid way through grating a lump of cheese. 'That means I'll have to cook something from scratch,' she muttered. She hurled the cheese back into the fridge and began pulling out packets of vegetables. Looking nervous, Dad backed his way out of the kitchen. Geena, Jazz and I followed him.

'Not so fast,' Auntie snapped, waving a bunch of dhania at us. 'You're helping.'

'Amber should do it,' Jazz grumbled, 'seeing as it's all down to her.'

'Yes, let Amber do the cooking,' Geena joined in. 'With any luck she might poison Molly and solve the problem.'

'What problem?' I said coolly, taking the dhania Auntie thrust at me in rather an unfriendly manner. 'We're helping someone. I don't see any problem with that.'

But underneath my ice-cool exterior, I was worried. I had really and truly started something. At this moment, I had absolutely no idea how it was all going to end.

CHAPTER 4

I wonder what it's like to be famous. No, that's not quite true. I wonder what it's like to be famous, and then, suddenly, not to be famous at all. To lose everything. To go back to being just an ordinary person in the street, someone nobody would look at twice. How would that feel? Could you ever go back to being normal again? And when it was all over, did you accept defeat gracefully or did you hope and believe that one day you would be famous all over again?

I snuggled down under the duvet and flipped through *OK!* magazine. It was full of soap stars, pop stars, actors and actresses. They were splitting up with their partners, getting married, having babies, talking about their latest film or book, or about their problems with alcohol or drugs or both. I frowned. It seemed that even when you were famous, you still had problems, just the same as everyone else. I would have liked to discuss it with Molly Mahal. But I had a strong feeling it was something she wouldn't want to talk about.

Jazz rolled over in bed and kicked my ankle. 'What are you looking so serious about?' she wanted to know.

'I was thinking about the fleeting nature of celebrity,' I said.

'Oh.' Jazz yawned. 'Are you going to make some tea?'

'No,' I replied. 'Make it yourself.'

Jazz pouted. 'I don't want to go downstairs,' she moaned. 'What if Molly Mahal's lurking about?'

I grinned. 'You're scared of her, aren't you?'

'No,' Jazz said indignantly.

'You are,' I chuckled. 'Honestly, Jazz, you *are* a fool.'

'Well, even if I was scared of her – which I'm not,' Jazz grumbled, '*you* ought to go and make the tea. Then you can take her a cup.'

'Don't be silly,' I said quickly. 'She's probably still asleep.'

Jazz giggled. '*You're* scared of her too, aren't you, Amber?'

'Oh, really!' I yawned delicately behind my hand. 'Of course I'm not.'

'You are,' Jazz said gleefully. 'I'm not surprised though. She's odd.'

We had managed to escape the curse of *Amir*

Ladka, Garib Ladka the previous day by pleading homework. Molly Mahal had watched Bollywood films all evening, and was still watching at midnight, long after the rest of us had gone to bed. I thought I'd heard footsteps coming upstairs around two o'clock in the morning, but I couldn't be sure.

'You'd be odd too if you were rich and famous and beautiful one minute, and poor and forgotten and downtrodden the next.' The more I thought about it, the more I was convinced that only a fool would crave being famous in the first place.

'I'd like to be famous,' Jazz said dreamily.

'Why?' I demanded.

'Well.' Jazz looked a bit confused. 'Everyone knows who you are.'

'That seems like an excellent reason,' I began sarcastically – but broke off to listen to Geena and Auntie arguing outside our bedroom door.

'I do *not* snore,' Geena was saying coldly.

'Yes, you do,' Auntie replied. 'It's like trying to sleep on the runway at Heathrow Airport.'

The door flew open and Geena marched in. Her face was red. 'This is all your fault, Amber,' she hissed. 'I didn't get a wink of sleep last night.'

'Neither did I,' grumbled Auntie, appearing behind her. She was wearing Geena's DKNY tartan pyjamas, which were slightly too small for her.

'At least I don't talk in my sleep,' Geena retorted.

Auntie looked a little nervous. 'I don't. Do I?'

'Oh yes.' Geena smiled. 'Don't worry, Auntie. I won't give away all your secrets.'

'I don't have any secrets to tell,' Auntie said. She seemed somewhat concerned all the same.

'Is Molly Mahal up yet?' I asked.

'She's sitting in the living room, wearing my second-best lengha,' Auntie said crossly. 'Go downstairs and make her a cup of tea, Amber. I don't think it would ever occur to her to boil the kettle herself.'

I groaned. 'Do I have to?'

'Oh yes,' said Auntie. 'And keep her down there as long as you can so I can grab some clothes from my room. I think she's left it unlocked. Otherwise I'm going to have to borrow something of Geena's.'

'Well, you're very welcome,' Geena said smoothly. 'Although, of course, I *am* a size smaller than you. You don't want to look ridiculous.'

Auntie retaliated with a loud, pig-like snore and whisked out of the room.

'What are you two staring at me for?' I asked.

'Auntie told you to go downstairs and make Molly Mahal a cup of tea,' Jazz reminded me, laughing uncontrollably.

'All right,' I said, trying to look unconcerned. 'I'm going.'

I climbed out of bed and began to dress, slowly. Geena jumped into my vacant spot, and she and Jazz lay there giggling under the duvet while I brushed my hair.

'You two are so childish,' I said. I went out of the bedroom, wishing I was somewhere far away.

The living-room door was shut. I had to take a deep breath before I could open it. Molly was sitting on the sofa, her back straight, the skirt of Auntie's peacock-blue lengha pooling around her on the carpet. The newsreader on TV was talking about someone who'd been shot in South London, but I don't think she was listening.

'Hi,' I said brightly. 'Did you sleep well?'

Molly turned to me. The unforgiving morning sun streaming through the windows highlighted the difference in her face; still beautiful, but not in the way it had been, and never would be again.

'I don't sleep that well these days,' she said quietly.

'Oh.' I wasn't actually scared of her. Not really. But there was something about her eyes. When she locked onto you, it was like being hit with the full force of her personality. You felt like a rabbit entranced by a snake. Well, I did, anyway.

I had no idea what to say next. Then I remembered why I was there. 'Tea?'

'Thank you.'

I scuttled out, feeling relieved. There were so many questions I wanted to ask her. How had she ended up in Reading? Why didn't she have any money? Wasn't there anyone who cared enough to help her out? But I couldn't ask any of these things. She seemed to have built a wall around herself which was impossible to penetrate.

I was standing by the boiling kettle, deep in thought, when the doorbell rang. I glanced at the kitchen clock. It was twenty past eight. A little early for visitors.

Mr Attwal stood outside, beaming at me. It was a shock. I'd never seen him away from the shop before. It was as if a polar bear had suddenly walked up our path and knocked on the door. Behind Mr Attwal was his shy little wife, Parmjit, who hardly ever said a word, or didn't get a chance to.

'Hello, Uncle,' I said, bewildered.

'Where is she?' Mr Attwal asked in a booming whisper.

'Who?' I asked stupidly.

'Molly Mahal.' Mr Attwal looked tremendously excited. 'You know, the film star. She *is* here, isn't she?'

I stifled a groan. If the news was already out, that meant *everybody* knew. You couldn't keep these things quiet. The Indian community has a better intelligence network than the CIA. Someone must have seen Molly arriving yesterday and done some detective work.

'Well, yes,' I admitted. Then regretted it instantly.

'See?' Mr Attwal turned triumphantly to his wife. 'It *is* true!'

'But she's not seeing anybody,' I broke in. 'She doesn't feel up to it.'

'Nonsense.' Mr Attwal swept me aside with one grand gesture. 'I was her biggest fan all those years ago. I thought about becoming a film star myself at one time but I didn't fancy the idea of wearing all that make-up. It's simply not very manly.'

'Shouldn't you be at the shop doing the Sunday newspapers?' I squeaked. But Mr Attwal was already bustling his way eagerly into our living room, his wife behind him.

I rushed after them. Maybe I was wrong. Molly might enjoy meeting some of her fans.

I was just in time to catch the look of absolute horror on Molly's face. And the abject disappointment on Mr Attwal's.

'Oh!' he breathed. 'I'd never have recognized you. I mean, pleased to meet you.'

Molly didn't reply. She snatched at her gold-fringed scarf and pulled it half across her face. Her hands were trembling. I realized that then her new-found confidence was as fragile as a butter-fly's wing.

Feeling horribly guilty, I dashed upstairs and bumped into Auntie coming out of the bedroom, her arms full of clothes.

'She's rearranged all my drawers,' she began indignantly.

'Ooh, that sounds painful,' Jazz giggled, popping her head out of our room.

'Who was at the door?' Dad grumbled, wandering out onto the landing in a pair of stripy pyjamas. 'At eight twenty a.m.? It's not natural.'

'Quick!' I whispered with urgency. 'It's Mr Attwal and his wife. They've come to see Molly Mahal.'

'You mean everyone knows she's here?' enquired Geena from behind Jazz.

'That's not good,' Jazz added.

'Oh my God,' Auntie groaned. 'I was hoping we could keep it quiet.'

'Maybe Mr Attwal hasn't told anyone else,' Dad began hopefully.

The doorbell rang.

'Don't answer it,' advised Jazz. 'They might go away.'

'There's someone at your door,' Mr Attwal roared from the living room. 'Shall I let them in?'

Auntie gritted her teeth. 'Amber, go and see who

it is,' she instructed. 'And the rest of you, get dressed. We're going to be busy this morning.'

I ran downstairs. As I passed the living room, I took a peek. Molly Mahal and the Attwals were sitting in complete silence. They were staring at her with curious eyes, and she was studiously ignoring them.

'Hello, *beti.*' Mrs Dhaliwal was at the door. Her buck-toothed son was standing next to her, shuffling his feet shyly. 'We've just popped round to say hello.'

'It's eight twenty-five,' I said. 'A.m.'

'Yes,' Mrs Dhaliwal agreed without a shred of embarrassment. She lived in the next street, and her great purpose in life was to get everybody married. She usually carried around a huge file full of the details of prospective marriage partners, although I couldn't see any sign of it this morning. 'Where is she then?'

'Who?' I asked, stalling.

Mrs Dhaliwal shook her finger playfully at me. 'Molly Mahal, of course.' She peered eagerly over my shoulder. 'We're dying to meet her. Aren't we, Sukhvinder?'

'I'm not sure that's a good idea—' I began.

Mrs Dhaliwal took not a bit of notice. She shoulder-charged past me into the house, dragging her son along by the wrist. He did at least look a bit embarrassed.

Cursing under my breath, I rushed along behind them, hoping to warn Molly Mahal. I was too late.

'Oh my.' Mrs Dhaliwal came to a full-stop in the living-room doorway, goggling at Molly Mahal from behind her thick spectacles. 'Haven't you *changed*.'

'That's exactly what I said,' Mr Attwal informed her in a loud whisper. 'Although she's still beautiful, of course. For her age.'

I was beginning to feel wretched. Mrs Dhaliwal plumped herself down on the sofa next to Molly Mahal without taking her eyes off her. Sukhvinder squeezed on too, looking mesmerized. Molly said nothing. She moved across to the other corner of the sofa, drawing her skirt around her.

'So' – Mrs Dhaliwal fixed her with an eager, beady stare – 'why have you been hiding yourself away all these years?'

I fled.

'Auntie!' I burst into Geena's bedroom. Auntie looked round, startled, halfway into her jeans. 'You've got to come downstairs.'

'What's going on?' she demanded.

'They're staring at her and she hates it.' I was upset – I didn't know why. 'And Mrs Dhaliwal's already started asking rude questions.'

'Oh no.' Auntie wriggled into her jeans and zipped them up. 'She'll be trying to get her married off next.'

'That might be a good thing,' remarked Geena, coming out of Jazz's room to see what was going on.

'Who'd have her?' Jazz whispered. 'It'd be worse than trying to find Auntie a husband.'

Dad joined us on the landing. 'Who's arrived now?' he asked crossly.

'Mrs Dhaliwal and Sukhvinder,' I replied.

'Oh no,' Geena said, trying to look disgusted. Sukhvinder has a big thing for her. Geena doesn't like him, but she likes him liking her, if you see what I mean.

'Don't worry,' I said as we all clattered downstairs. 'He's only got eyes for Molly Mahal at the moment.'

This time Geena genuinely did look disgusted. Especially as Sukhvinder didn't even glance up as we crowded into the living room. The temperature in there had dropped so much, it was below freezing. You could have picked up a knife and sliced the tension.

'Of course, it's not always easy to find a husband at your age,' Mrs Dhaliwal was saying helpfully. 'You know, our men don't want wives who are a little old to be having children, hmm?'

I could gladly have hit her. Geena and Jazz gasped. Auntie looked uncomfortable and Dad annoyed. I don't know if they noticed the fleeting look of pain that crossed Molly Mahal's face. But I did.

'But if we could find you a nice, divorced guy . . .' Mrs Dhaliwal tapped her teeth thoughtfully with a manicured fingernail. 'Yes. Someone who's already had their children. Now, what kind of men do you like?'

'Good morning, *bhaibh-ji*,' Auntie cut in swiftly. I could have kissed her. 'Hello, everybody.' She didn't wait for them to reply. 'Lovely to see you all. Now let's have tea.' She turned to Molly. 'Are you ready? Johnny's going to drop you off at your friend's house right away.'

I breathed a sigh of relief. Thank goodness for Auntie. Not something I would say very often, of course.

'I am?' Dad looked puzzled, then got it. 'Oh, yes. So I am.'

'No tea for us.' Looking disappointed, Mrs Dhaliwal heaved herself off the sofa. 'Come along, Sukhvinder.' She had to repeat herself twice before he could finally tear his gaze away from Molly. 'I'll be back,' she threatened, waddling over to the door. 'And next time I'll bring my marriage file.'

'Yes, you must tell us more about the *filmi*

industry some time,' Mr Attwal chimed in. He went reluctantly to the living-room door, his wife scuttling after him. Dad, Auntie, Geena, Jazz and I escorted them out, forming a barrier so they couldn't get back in.

'You know,' Mr Attwal said thoughtfully, 'she could still make films if she wanted to.'

'Oh no.' Mrs Dhaliwal looked shocked. 'She's much too old to play the heroine now.'

'Of course she is,' Mr Attwal agreed. 'But she could play the hero's mother. Or his sister. You know, minor roles like that.'

I winced at the loudness of his tone and pulled the door shut behind me.

As Dad, Auntie, Geena and Jazz edged Mrs Dhaliwal and the others down the hall towards the front door, I went back into the living room. Molly Mahal sat there, a frozen look on her face.

'Are you all right?' I blurted out.

'Yes, why shouldn't I be?' she replied coldly. But her hands were still shaking slightly.

'Well . . .' I began awkwardly. 'I suppose it's nice that people want to meet you.' I was going to say *after all these years*, but stopped myself in time.

Molly shook her head. 'They don't want to meet me,' she said. 'They're just desperate to see how awful I look.'

'That's not true,' I said, very weakly. 'Anyway,

you look lovely.' I just managed not to add *for your age*. Every time I opened my mouth, I seemed eager to stick my foot in it.

Geena popped her head round the door. 'Guess who's here,' she groaned. 'Uncle Dave, Auntie Rita, Baby and Biji.'

'You mean—?' I glanced over at Molly.

Geena nodded and ducked out again.

'Look, you don't have to see anybody if you don't want to,' I said quickly. 'You could always go up to your room.'

'Really.' Molly looked at me levelly. 'I thought meeting your friends and relatives was the price I had to pay for staying here.'

'No,' I said, shocked. 'Not at all.'

Molly sighed. 'Amber,' she said flatly, 'there's always a price to pay.' And stayed where she was.

'Someone will have to talk to her.' Auntie slammed a plate of toast down on the table. 'Find out what her plans are. We can't go on like this.'

I didn't dare reply. Neither did Geena and Jazz. We kept our heads down over our breakfast plates. Auntie was in the mother of all moods, and for once I could not blame her.

Sunday had been a truly terrible day. Visitors had come and gone until late evening. They'd drunk our tea, eaten all our food and sat and stared at Molly Mahal. Some of them had been too over-awed to say anything. Like Mrs Macey, who hadn't been able to stand it any longer and had crept round in the late morning to find out exactly what was going on. But our relatives had been the most badly behaved of them all.

'So where is she then?' Uncle Dave had boomed, rubbing his hands together as he stepped into the hall.

'Ssh!' I said, as did Dad, Auntie, Geena and Jazz.

'We've heard all about her, you know,' Auntie Rita chattered eagerly, waving her hands around and setting her expensive gold bracelets jangling. 'She's supposed to be hideous now. Is she?'

'I'm not surprised,' sniffed Biji, leaning heavily on her walking stick. 'That's what comes of being a *filmi* actress. The movies are full of immorality.'

'She's got to be pretty ancient, too,' Baby chimed in. She was playing the good little Indian girl today, wearing a pink and white lengha, but a good deal of tummy and cleavage was on show. 'She must be forty at least.'

'And how are you, Poonam *beti*?' Auntie en-quired silkily. 'You didn't catch a cold yesterday after all? That was lucky.'

Baby's eyes narrowed and she said no more.

That set the scene for the rest of the visit. Biji limped into our living room, stared at Molly Mahal and announced, 'Well! How the mighty are fallen.' Uncle Davinder couldn't take his eyes off her, and announced in a very audible whisper to Dad that although she wasn't a patch on how she'd looked before, she wasn't bad at all. Meanwhile, all Auntie Rita wanted to know was if Baby had any potential as a Bollywood star.

'People have told us that she's so beautiful, we ought to let her take a screen test,' she said with a tinkling laugh as Baby simpered beside her. 'Of course, we'd never actually allow her to do it.'

'Of course not,' Biji growled, tapping her stick sharply on the floor. 'Actresses have no morals. No family values. No decent, respectable, clean-living girl would want to enter such a profession.'

Molly looked Baby up and down. 'In that case, I think she'd be perfect,' she said coolly.

I'd had to leave the room so that I could laugh as noiselessly as possible in the kitchen. Geena and Jazz had joined me, gasping for breath. Even Dad and Auntie had struggled not to look amused.

From that moment on, though, something about Molly Mahal slowly started to change. She didn't hide behind her scarf when new visitors arrived. Instead, she stared them full in the face, daring them to make comments about how much she'd changed. Once they'd looked into those eyes, many of them were too mesmerized to say a word. Or too scared. By the end of the long, tiring day, I had the feeling that she'd faced up to herself, and to the ordeal of all those curious, staring eyes, and she'd won through. Secretly I felt quite proud of her.

But now, the next morning, we were back at square one. Molly Mahal was still here. We were no further forward in finding out what she was going to do, when she was planning to leave. She was still our responsibility.

'You heard what Auntie said, Amber.' Geena nudged me. 'Someone's got to talk to her.'

'She didn't mean me,' I said in a low voice. I hoped she didn't because I had no intention of doing it. I'd never been so glad that Monday morning at school was looming ahead of me, science test and all.

'She'll have to go *soon*,' said Jazz through a mouthful of toast. 'No one could be so thick-skinned as to stay somewhere they're not wanted.'

'They might if they haven't anywhere else to go,' I said.

Jazz didn't reply. She looked a little ashamed of herself.

At this moment, Dad rushed into the kitchen wearing his best pinstriped suit. He had two ties in his hand, one a deep crimson, the other pink with blue chevrons.

'Which one looks best, do you think?' he asked anxiously, holding the ties up against his white shirt.

'Dad, what's the matter with you?' Geena asked with amusement. 'I thought you usually just put on the first tie you pick up.'

Dad looked awkward. 'I want to look my best for once.'

'Why?' Jazz asked.

'Oh, never mind that.' Auntie brandished a buttery knife threateningly. 'Johnny, we have to talk.'

'We do?' Dad asked absently, weighing up the ties, one in each hand.

Auntie sighed loudly. I put down my cereal spoon. This was going to be fun.

'Of course we do,' said Auntie, looking exasperated. 'About – you know.' She rolled her eyes upwards. We could hear Molly moving around upstairs.

Dad looked puzzled. 'We have to talk about the ceiling?' he asked.

'Someone's going to be assaulted with the butter knife very soon,' said Geena in a low voice.

'Molly Mahal!' Auntie muttered savagely. 'What are we going to *do*?'

'Well' – Dad frowned – 'nothing, for the moment.'

'Nothing!' Auntie gasped in horror. Geena and

Jazz groaned theatrically. I was staying out of it.

'What *can* we do?' Dad pointed out, very reasonably, I thought. 'After all, the girls invited her to stay—'

'That's not quite true,' Geena broke in. She and Jazz eyed me with great bitterness.

'Well, never mind.' Dad took a piece of toast. 'Whatever happened, she's now our guest.'

'But she can't stay here for ever,' said Auntie plaintively.

'Of course not,' Dad agreed. 'But the girls want her to go to the school party, don't they? So I think it's only fair that she stays with us until then, especially as she doesn't seem to have anywhere else to go.'

Auntie's jaw dropped so far it almost hit the breakfast table. 'But – but,' she stammered, 'that's four weeks away!'

'Well, that gives her plenty of time to sort out some other living arrangements, doesn't it?' Dad raised his eyebrows. 'We can't just turn her out onto the streets.'

'No, we can't,' I chimed in. That won me several more killer looks.

'But the girls haven't even asked her about the party yet,' said Auntie in a disgruntled voice. 'She might not want to do it.'

'Well, ask her today,' Dad said calmly, but there

was more than a hint of steel in his voice. 'Then we can decide where we go from there.'

I wondered if he'd been reading Kim's *How to Say No and Mean It!* I couldn't remember him being this assertive – oh – for months. Since before Mum.

'And now we've sorted that out' – Dad held up both ties again – 'which one do you think? The red or the pink?'

'The red.'

No one had heard Molly Mahal come downstairs. She stood in the doorway, wearing another of Auntie's suits, a silver and turquoise one this time, with some rather pretty beaten-silver jewellery and glittery sea-green bangles.

'It looks better with that suit,' she went on, smiling at Dad. 'Very smart.'

'Why, thank you,' Dad said. He seemed flustered but pleased. He put the red tie on, grabbed his briefcase and went out, looking ten feet tall.

Auntie sighed. I think she knew that she was beaten for the time being. But I was sure she wouldn't be giving up that easily.

'Frosties?' she said coolly, plonking the box down in front of Molly Mahal.

'Aren't you making dosas?' Molly asked, with a delicate frown. 'Or puri?'

Auntie shook her head. 'Feel free to make them yourself,' she replied.

Molly laughed, a tinkling musical sound. 'Oh dear, *I* don't know how to cook,' she said with incredulous amusement. 'My chef and my maids did everything for me.' She raised her eyebrows and looked at Auntie. There was a challenge in her eyes.

Geena and Jazz sat up, waiting for the storm to break. I watched with interest to see if steam would actually come out of Auntie's ears. It looked as though it might.

'Well,' she began with cutting emphasis, '*I'm* not your—'

'Come on, girls,' I broke in brightly. 'We'd better be going too.' It was still early, but I was desperate to get away.

'Wait!' Auntie pleaded. She looked quite distraught at the idea of being left with Molly all day. Once again, I couldn't blame her. They seemed to strike sparks off each other whenever they were in the same room. 'Geena hasn't finished her breakfast.'

Geena looked down at her empty cereal bowl. 'Well, unless I'm going to eat the cutlery, I think I'm done.'

'I could eat an egg,' Molly broke in, eyeballing Auntie haughtily across the table. She seemed able to switch from sweet to snooty in one blink of an eye. 'Soft-boiled, with one piece of toast. *If* it's no trouble.'

They stared each other out. Words trembled on Auntie's lips as Geena, Jazz and I watched, fascinated. Then she gave a sigh that seemed to come from the depths of her toes, opened the fridge and took out a box of eggs.

'Kim's here, girls,' Dad called from the hall.

'Kim?' I frowned, pushing my chair back. 'What's she doing here?' She didn't call for us. We usually met up on the way to school.

Kim rushed into the kitchen, *How to Say No and Mean It!* tucked under her arm, her face eager, her eyes out on stalks. She came to a dead halt when she saw us all at the table, flushing bright red from her neck to the roots of her hair.

'Oh!' she gasped, staring at Molly. 'Are *you* the famous film star?'

Molly smiled graciously. 'I am Molly Mahal,' she said, and held out her hand. Kim took it reverently. For a minute I thought she was going to kiss it.

'How did you know she was here, Kim?' I asked. I had to repeat the question twice.

'Our neighbours the Chowdhurys were talking about it. Their son Miki works for *Masala Express*.' Kim immediately turned her attention back to Molly. 'You're very beautiful,' she blurted out. She was so dazzled she dropped her book. It landed on Jazz's toe.

I don't think Kim could have said anything that would have pleased Molly more. She gave Kim a very satisfied smile.

'What are you reading?' she enquired, turning the full beam of those amazing eyes onto her.

Kim fumbled to pick up the book, banging her head on the table and stepping back onto Jazz's other foot. 'Oh . . .' she said breathlessly. 'Just this.'

Molly studied the blurb. '"Become the confident person you've always wanted to be. Learn how to get what you want. Take control of your life and learn how to make people do whatever you want them to."' She laughed. 'I've never had a problem with that.'

'That figures,' Auntie muttered.

'Perhaps I should give you some assertiveness training, Kim,' Molly suggested playfully.

Kim, the fool, looked thrilled. 'Oh, I'd love it!' she gasped, clasping her hands.

'That's all we need,' I whispered to Geena. 'Another diva.'

The doorbell rang.

'I'll get it.' Grumbling, Jazz limped over to the door. We heard a murmur of voices. A moment later Mrs Macey crept into the kitchen, looking terrified but excited. She was followed, incredibly, by Leo. He was clutching Dad's *Daily Telegraph* in his hand.

'Hey, this is getting better,' I said, smiling at him. 'Personal service.'

Annoyingly, Leo ignored me. He was staring at Molly Mahal with a look on his face that was becoming tiresomely familiar. A look of rapt enchantment.

'I thought Miss Mahal might like some of my home-made strawberry jam,' Mrs Macey squeaked. She produced a jar from behind her back, holding it out.

'Oh, how kind,' said Molly. 'Thank you.' She turned her dazzling gaze to Leo. 'And who's this?'

'This is Leo,' I said grumpily. 'He's our paperboy. As you can see, he loves his job so much he actually brings the newspapers into our house and delivers them personally.'

Leo ignored me. 'Hello,' he said, spellbound.

All this attention was having an effect on Molly Mahal. She was beginning to blossom like a flower unfurling its petals.

'Do sit down.' She clicked her fingers in Auntie's direction. 'We'll have tea.'

I could almost see Auntie's blood pressure rising like mercury in a thermometer.

'Well, of all the—' she began.

The doorbell rang again.

'I wonder who this can be,' said Jazz.

'Well, whoever it is,' I muttered bitterly, 'you can be sure they won't be coming to see *us*.'

Mrs Macey, Kim and Leo were now comfortably seated at the kitchen table with Molly. They were hanging on her every word and gesture with fascinated faces.

'Oh dear,' said Geena. 'I think our Amber's got a touch of the green-eyed monster.'

Jazz giggled.

'Will somebody please answer the door?' Auntie snapped.

I slipped out of the kitchen. More than ever, I was wondering what I'd got us into. And how everything was going to end. Molly Mahal seemed able to entrance everyone and wrap them tightly round her little finger. Even Dad had fallen under her spell if he was prepared to let her stay until the school party . . .

I opened the door and almost fell over with shock.

Mr Arora was outside. He looked slightly embarrassed and boyishly eager.

'Sir!' I croaked. 'What are you doing here?' But I already knew.

'Amber, so sorry to bother you this early in the morning,' he began. 'But I was on my way to school, and – well – I had to come and find out if it was true—'

'Yes, it's true,' I said wearily.

Mr Arora's big, dark eyes grew dreamy. 'Oh, Molly was my favourite star when I was a kid,' he murmured. 'She looked fantastic in *Amir Ladka, Garib Ladka*. Rubbish film, but she was beautiful.' He looked hopefully at me with big brown eyes. 'Can I meet her?'

'Sir' – I felt I had to warn him – 'she's a lot older now. She doesn't look quite the same.'

'Yes, I understand.' Mr Arora wasn't about to shoulder-charge me aside, as Mrs Dhaliwal had done, but he was edging his way forward. 'I don't expect her to. What's she doing here anyway? Are your family friends of hers?'

'Not quite.' I grinned, thinking of Auntie. 'We just heard that she was living close by, and decided it might be a good idea to invite her to the school's Bollywood party.'

Mr Arora looked thrilled. 'What a fantastic idea!'

'But we haven't actually asked her yet.'

Mr Arora wasn't listening. He had homed in on voices coming from the kitchen, and was heading towards them at speed.

He opened the kitchen door. Auntie gasped and dropped the box of tea bags. Geena and Jazz looked stunned. So did Kim.

Mr Arora ignored them all. He only had eyes for one person. 'I can't believe it's really you,' he breathed, moving forward as if in a trance. 'It's a privilege and a pleasure to meet you.'

For a fleeting second, Molly looked uncertain. Then she brightened visibly as she took in, at a glance, the genuine admiration in Mr Arora's eyes, as well as his dark good looks. She rose and held out her hand. 'And I'm delighted to meet you,' she purred kittenishly.

I thought I could hear Auntie muttering under her breath as she scooped up tea bags. 'This is my teacher, Mr Arora,' I said.

'You're a teacher?' Molly arched her eyebrows. 'I'm amazed. Have you never thought of screen-testing for the movies?'

'Oh, please,' Auntie muttered.

Mr Arora blushed with delight. 'I can't tell you how thrilled I am.' He slid into one of the chairs without taking his eyes off her. 'You're as beautiful as I remember,' he added gallantly. It was a lie, but a brave one all the same.

'Tea?' Auntie snapped, shoving the box of dusty tea bags under Mr Arora's nose.

He didn't even look at her. 'No, thank you.'

Auntie flounced over to the kettle.

'Haven't you got two paper rounds to finish?' I said pointedly to Leo.

'Yes,' he replied, not moving.

Mr Arora seemed unable to tear his gaze from

Molly's mesmerizing brown eyes. 'I know this is probably a real nerve,' he began shyly, 'but we're having a Bollywood-themed party at the end of term. It would be wonderful if you would be our guest of honour.'

Molly's eyes narrowed and she drew her breath in sharply. 'No, I don't think so—' she began.

'Oh, please,' Mr Arora broke in. 'Won't you at least consider it?'

Molly frowned. I could make a guess at what she was thinking. She wanted to continue dazzling Mr Arora, but the thought of all those curious people staring at her and gossiping about her decline, maybe raking up all the old scandal and history, was too much.

'You heard what she said,' Auntie cut in. 'She's not interested. Anyway, the Bollywood party isn't for weeks yet' – she faced Molly with a full-on, challenging stare – 'and she'll probably have left long before then.'

'Well, there's no harm in asking,' Mr Arora said, almost sharply.

He and Auntie looked hard at each other. It was almost, but not quite, a glare.

'Oh, please come to the party,' Kim said earnestly. 'It won't be the same without you.'

'Can anyone come, or do you have to be a pupil at the school?' Leo wanted to know.

'I'll help with the preparations,' Mrs Macey offered.

Molly Mahal flicked Mr Arora a look from under long, sooty lashes. 'Well, I'll think about it,' she said huskily.

'Great!' Mr Arora beamed with pleasure. He was so dazzled by Molly, I don't think he would have noticed if Auntie had thrown the box of tea bags at him.

Geena and Jazz closed in on me from either side.

'Ooh, this is getting interesting,' Jazz whispered.

'Yes,' Geena agreed. 'How long before Auntie strangles Molly Mahal? Place your bets now.'

I nodded. It seemed that if Auntie wanted Mr Arora, she was going to have to put up a bit of a fight. Jazz was so right. Things were about to get very interesting.

CHAPTER 5

'About this film star . . .' began George Botley.

'George.' I put my hands on my hips and eyed him with aggression. 'Never mention that subject to me again.'

George looked aggrieved. 'I just want to know if she's coming to the Bollywood party or not.'

'I'm warning you, George.' I took a step forward. 'Please go away before I'm forced to kill you with my bare hands.'

'She means it, George,' Jazz added.

George pulled a face. He shambled off across the school playground muttering, 'Women!'

'And that goes for anyone else who wants to ask me about film stars and Bollywood parties,' I said, shooting looks like daggers at everyone around me. Chelsea and Sharelle, who were heading in our direction, swerved aside. They hurried off, pretending to be discussing maths homework.

'Calm down, Amber,' Geena advised me. 'You're losing it.'

'Sorry.' I took a breath. 'It's been a long week.'

Molly Mahal had been living with us for seven days. It was true that we had been at school for most of that time so we didn't have to see her. But arriving home in the evenings had become one long ordeal. Auntie would be lurking behind the front door, waiting to escort us into the kitchen and reel off a long list of complaints. Apparently, Molly didn't do anything except sit around the house all day, have baths, watch films and change into different outfits. She didn't know how to cook, use a vacuum cleaner or do the ironing. Or so she said. She had Auntie wearing a path to Mr Basra's video store to borrow more movies. Yesterday a reporter from *Masala Express* had turned up on the doorstep. Molly had had a fit, and Auntie had been forced to shoo him away with a broom. Oh, Auntie had tale after tale to tell us.

Living with Molly was a rollercoaster ride. Sometimes she would be sweet as apple pie. That was if she got what she wanted immediately. If she didn't, within seconds she'd turn into the biggest Bollywood diva going, and you could see the steel behind the sweet smile.

Whatever Molly wanted, Molly seemed to get.

Dad seemed more friendly with her than any of us, though. From him we found out that Molly had come to England when her career ended to stay with an old aunt. After her aunt died, she was on her own and living off her savings. When they were gone, she'd started selling her belongings and jewellery.

'Why didn't she claim income support?' Auntie wanted to know. 'And housing benefit?'

'She went to the Social Security offices, and the Indian guy behind the desk recognized her,' Dad explained. 'She was so humiliated, she never went back.'

Listening to this, Geena, Jazz and I were silent. Lifting the curtain on someone's life and taking a peek behind it tells you all sorts of things you never dreamed. We did feel very sorry for her.

But that did not make her one bit easier to live with.

And now . . .

Word had got round at school (I suspected Kim, Mr Arora and all the Indian pupils, frankly) that a Bollywood film star was staying at our house and might be persuaded to be the guest of honour at our party. At least half the school had never heard of her, but they were dead excited anyway. Everyone wanted daily updates about what was happening. It was sending me slowly mad. Or slowly sending me mad. Whatever.

'Girls!' Mr Arora had exited the school building

and was bearing down on us, his face eager. No escape was possible. 'Any news about Molly?'

'No,' I said, as rudely as I dared.

'Oh.' Mr Arora looked enormously disappointed.

'Ah, there you are, Jai.' The head of the lower school, Mr Grimwade, bounced out of the school office and headed towards us. For a man composed almost entirely of circles, he was very light on his feet. 'And our Bollywood girls! I was hoping to have a word with you about this film star.'

I ground my teeth together.

'Easy, Amber,' Geena whispered.

'Has she decided yet if she's coming to the party?' Mr Grimwade looked at us hopefully.

'No, sir,' replied Jazz. I didn't trust myself.

'Oh. Pity. Well, keep trying.' Mr Grimwade was becoming more desperate as the days went by. I guessed that Mr Morgan, our free-spending headmaster, was making his life a misery. 'Now . . .' Mr Grimwade went on, studying the clipboard he was clutching. 'Do I have your forms for the sponsored walk next week?'

'Yes, sir,' we chorused glumly.

'And don't forget we're collecting aluminium drinks cans too,' he added. 'There's a prize for the class which collects the most. A new whiteboard.'

'Whoopee,' I said under my breath.

'I hope your aunt hasn't forgotten about the

meeting after school today?' enquired Mr Arora, as Mr Grimwade flipped through the huge sheaf of papers again. 'We've got a good many things to sort out before the party. We need to divide up the jobs between our volunteers.'

'Oh, she'll be there,' I assured him. 'So will we.'

Mr Arora looked even more eager. 'Maybe Molly Mahal will come with her.'

'I wouldn't bank on it,' I said in a wet-blanket kind of voice.

'Oh yes, I wanted to ask you about Kyra Hollins.' Mr Grimwade looked up from the clipboard. 'You're a friend of hers, aren't you, Geena? I don't seem to have her form for the sponsored walk.'

'That's because she's broken her leg, sir,' replied Geena. 'She tripped over a pile of aluminium cans she'd collected.'

'Ah.' Mr Grimwade tapped his pen against his bald forehead. 'Will she be able to do the sponsored walk next week or not then?'

'I should think so,' Geena said solemnly. 'Providing she's allowed to hop.'

'Yes.' Mr Grimwade nodded slowly. 'A sponsored hop. That sounds like rather a good idea . . .' He beckoned to Mr Arora and they went inside.

'Wouldn't it be great,' Jazz said, 'if we had a time machine?'

'Oh, you mean we could go back in time and

stop Amber from having such terrible ideas?' Geena took up the tale.

'Yes,' said Jazz. 'How useful would that be?'

'Quiet,' I said irritably. I'd just spotted Kim coming in through the school gates, and my mood was not improving. She was enchanted by Molly Mahal, and talked about her constantly.

'Why didn't you wait for me this morning?' Kim asked, somewhat over-assertively in my opinion.

'We left early because Auntie was in a foul temper,' I said grumpily.

'Oh dear.' Kim stared at me quizzically. 'She's not the only one, is she?'

'Amber's not feeling herself today,' Geena interrupted.

'Who's she feeling then?' Jazz sniggered. I flicked her ear. 'Ow!'

'How's Molly Mahal?' Kim asked in a worshipping tone.

'Don't mention Molly Mahal or Bollywood parties,' I warned her. 'Not now. Not ever.'

'But—'

'No.' I shook my head. 'I'm saying no and meaning it.'

'There is no way Molly Mahal will come to the Bollywood party,' Jazz said. 'So why do you think she doesn't just leave?'

School was over and we were on our way to the meeting in the new building. As ever, we were stunned and envious when we crossed the road and entered the upper school. It was a revelation. Everything was clean and bright and sparkling new there. The floors were polished wood. The classrooms were well equipped, carpeted and spacious. The lights worked.

'I really don't know,' I replied, running my finger along the clean cream paintwork of the wide, sunny corridor. 'But she seems a lot more cheerful these days, what with Mrs Macey, Kim and Mr Arora chasing around after her,' I added bitterly.

'You forgot Leo,' Geena reminded me. 'I heard him telling her about his brother the other day. And didn't he bring her a free copy of *Masala Express*?'

'Don't get wound up, Amber,' Jazz said kindly. 'She's way too old for him.'

I sniffed. 'As if I care.'

The meeting was happening in the new school hall, a huge architect's dream of a building made of concrete, glass and steel. When we arrived, Mr Arora and Ms Woods, head of drama, were setting out chairs in a semicircle. Mr Grimwade was standing on the sidelines ordering them about. There were several other teachers there – Miss Patel (geography); Miss Véronique, the French student teacher; Mr Lucas, Jazz's form teacher; and Mr Hernandez (French and Spanish), who everyone was convinced was mad after he broke into a flamenco dance at a governors' meeting. He said it was a great stress-reliever.

Besides us, there were about fifteen other pupils hanging around, many of them looking disgruntled. I guess Mr Arora had used the term 'volunteer' quite loosely. Startlingly, one of them was Kim.

'What are you doing here?' I asked.

Kim shrugged, turning delicately pink. 'I volunteered to help,' she said.

'You didn't say anything before,' I accused her.

Kim looked sheepish. I should possibly have probed a bit more, but it didn't occur to me. Not then.

'Let's make a start,' boomed Mr Grimwade, glancing at his watch. 'I have a meeting with Mr Morgan in half an hour.'

'Hello, everyone.' Auntie came through the double doors, looking casually glamorous in a pale-blue shalwar kameez. She had the look of someone who'd made a huge effort with her appearance but was pretending she hadn't. 'I'm not late, am I?'

'Not at all,' said Mr Grimwade jovially. 'And how is the star of our show?'

Auntie smiled. 'I'm fine, thank you.'

'Er – I meant Miss Mahal,' Mr Grimwade mumbled.

'Oh, her.' Auntie's tone was clipped. 'She's sitting in our living room, watching one of her own films. As you do.'

'We thought she might come with you,' Mr Arora chipped in.

'Well, she didn't,' Auntie said glacially.

'Did you ask her?' Mr Arora wanted to know.

I glanced at Geena and Jazz. This was getting dangerous.

'Shall we begin?' Mr Grimwade cut in impatiently.

We sat down. It was interesting to see that Mr Arora and Auntie chose chairs as far away from each other as possible. In fact, Auntie deliberately crossed the room, pushing her way past several other people to sit next to me and Kim.

'Was that strictly necessary?' I asked.

'I don't know what you mean, Amber,' Auntie said distantly. 'Hello, Kim.'

'You'll never get your hooks into him if you treat him like that,' Jazz muttered.

'I strongly object to that phrase,' Auntie snapped. 'I don't intend to "get my hooks" into anyone.'

'Well, you should,' said Jazz stubbornly. 'You'll never find anyone as good as Mr Arora.'

Auntie glared at her.

'I call this meeting to order,' said Mr Grimwade pompously. 'Now, I know that Mr Arora and Miss Dhillon have been co-ordinating the arrangements for the party up till now' – Auntie and Mr Arora gave each other a cool glance – 'but we can't expect them to do all the work. That's why we're here, to divide up the rest of the tasks. And may I just say how pleased I am to see so many of you. It's marvellous that fundraising fatigue is not an issue at Coppergate School!'

He paused as if he was expecting a rousing cheer of agreement. There wasn't one.

'The headmaster told me I had to come,' said Mr Hernandez.

'So I'm going to ask Miss Dhillon and Mr Arora to give us an update,' Mr Grimwade swept on regardless. 'Then we can see where help is required. Miss Dhillon?'

Auntie flipped open her handbag and took out a list. 'Everything's under control,' she said briskly. 'I've made a list of the food we'll require. Samosas, bhajis, pakoras, jelabis, barfi and so on. We're asking the parents to cook food and send it in.' She shot a challenging glance at Mr Arora. 'I believe a letter is going home with the pupils tonight.'

Mr Arora nodded, equally coolly. 'We're also

asking for donations of fairy lights and coloured tinsel to decorate the hall,' he added. 'And the lower school will be making other decorations, as well as posters to publicize the event.'

'There go our art classes for the next three weeks,' Jazz grumbled.

'I've been in touch with Mr Basra at the local video shop and he's promised us some Bollywood posters,' Auntie went on. 'And I was hoping we might get a local DJ to do the music. I've heard Chapati MC is very good.'

'He is,' said Geena. 'He's gorgeous as well,' she whispered in my ear.

'We could have a performance by a bhangra group,' suggested Miss Patel. 'I could ask Amit Sagoo in my class. His dad's a bhangra dancer.'

'That's a good idea,' Auntie agreed. We all nodded.

Mr Arora cleared his throat. I don't know why, but I could sense trouble coming.

'Can I just say that, though this all sounds excellent, I think we should really be discussing the most important issue.'

'And what is that?' Auntie enquired icily.

'Whether we can persuade Molly Mahal to attend the party,' Mr Arora replied with spirit. 'I do feel it would be an amazing coup for us if she agreed to come. It would generate a lot of interest among the Asian community, and we'd probably have a sell-out event on our hands.'

'You've asked her,' Auntie ground out from between gritted teeth. 'She said no. I think we should move on.'

'She said she'd *think* about it,' Mr Arora retorted stubbornly. 'I'm sure we can persuade her. Maybe we could offer her some kind of incentive to attend.'

'What is he going to do?' Geena whispered. 'Ask her to marry him?'

'You don't mean *pay* her?' Mr Grimwade looked aghast.

'I agree with Mr Arora,' said a timid but assertive voice to my left. Everyone turned to stare at Kim, not least me. 'I think we should do our best to get her to come.'

'So do I,' Miss Patel put in. 'We'd definitely sell loads more tickets. And I'm dying to meet her myself.' She turned to Mr Hernandez next to her and whispered, 'She's supposed to be hideous now, you know.'

'Really?' said Mr Hernandez. 'In that case, maybe we should pay her to stay away.'

Kim flushed. 'She's not hideous at all,' she said defensively. 'She's very beautiful.'

'Yes, she is,' said Mr Arora with vigour.

Auntie muttered something inaudible.

'Well, we can't wait much longer,' Mr Grimwade

pointed out. 'If she *is* coming, we'll need to publicize it. The posters will be going up in the next week or two.'

'Leave it with me,' said Mr Arora confidently. 'I'll do my best to persuade her.'

'Can you hear that noise?' I murmured in Geena's ear. 'It's the sound of Auntie's blood pressure rising.'

Somehow Auntie managed to keep it together for the rest of the meeting, which, luckily, wasn't very long. She didn't say goodbye to Mr Arora when we left.

'Are you all right, Auntie?' I asked as we crossed the playground to the car park. Kim was trailing along behind us, beaming after making her astonishing stand.

'I'm fine,' Auntie snapped, pointing her keys at the car. 'Why on earth wouldn't I be?'

'Because that's Miss Patel's car you're trying to unlock,' I said. 'She's got the same silver Golf as you.'

Auntie skirted round Miss Patel's car, cursing under her breath.

'I've never done anything like that before,' Kim babbled gaily. 'I hate speaking in public. Do you think I sounded nervous?'

'What do you want, marks out of ten?' I asked. Then instantly regretted it as Kim's face dropped.

'We don't have the time to hang around waiting for Madam Mahal to make up her mind,' Auntie muttered grimly under her breath. We all climbed into the car and she threw it into gear. 'Why can't they see that?'

'Wait!' Jazz shrieked as the car moved off. 'I'm not in properly yet.'

Auntie braked with unnecessary vigour, and we all lurched forward. 'It's ridiculous. She's said she doesn't want to do it. Why can't they just accept it?'

'Remind me again why we went to see Molly Mahal,' Geena remarked to me under her breath. 'I seem to remember it was going to earn us all sorts of praise from Auntie.'

'Ha ha ha,' said Jazz savagely. I judged it best to keep quiet.

Auntie drove off at speed.

'And another thing,' she began again, coming to an emergency stop outside the block of flats where Kim lived. 'We *still* don't know when she's going to leave.'

'Er – do you mind if I come home with you?' Kim asked timidly, staying where she was.

I leaned over the seats to eyeball her. 'Are you coming to see Molly?'

'Well . . .' Kim began, shrivelling under my probing gaze.

'Oh, go on,' I said cuttingly. 'You might as well be assertive and tell the truth.'

'Well, I did promise Miss Mahal I'd visit her today,' Kim mumbled.

'Fair enough,' I said coolly.

We drove on in simmering silence. All of us were stressed. Auntie seemed to feel that she'd given away something of how she felt about Mr Arora. Now she'd shut up like a clam. Geena and Jazz were depressed, as I was. Kim looked defiant, which didn't suit her one bit. I was quite sure I would have to have a serious word with her at some point.

'Who's nicked my parking space?' Auntie demanded irritably as we drew up outside the house. I had a strong suspicion that she would leap out of the car and positively enjoy throttling them to death, whoever they were.

A white van was parked in 'our' space. BEENA'S BOUQUETS – FLOWERS FOR THAT SPECIAL OCCASION was printed on the side of the van in big bold letters.

We all peered out of the car windows. A woman in a green sari was at our front door, handing over an enormous bouquet of flowers to Molly Mahal. Even from this distance I could see that the flowers weren't cheap and ordinary. These were sumptuous, hot-housed blooms, wrapped in palest candy-pink tissue paper.

Auntie fidgeted in her seat until the florist had driven off, then shot the car into the empty space. Kim was out and up the path first. Molly Mahal was still on the step, her arms filled with flowers, looking oh so very pleased with herself.

'Aren't they lovely?' Kim breathed.

I followed her to take a look. Pale pink and white rosebuds, white lilies and blue irises. It was a ravishing bouquet.

'Who sent it?' asked Auntie from behind me. She sounded a touch strained.

Molly Mahal produced a tiny cream card with a flourish. '"Please do consider coming to our party,"' she read out. '"We'd love you to be the guest of honour! With best wishes, Jai Arora."'

I gasped. Partly because of the shock and partly because Geena had just poked me violently in the back. Jazz immediately turned to stare at Auntie with saucer eyes.

'Mr Arora!' Kim said with delight. 'He must really like you.'

'Evidently,' said Auntie in a freezing tone, pushing past Molly Mahal and into the house.

'Could you put them in water for me?' With a dazzling smile, Molly thrust the bouquet into Auntie's arms as she passed. Auntie took the flowers meekly and didn't say a word. She looked quite upset, although she was doing her best to hide it.

'Well,' said Geena when Molly and Kim had followed Auntie inside. 'What do you make of that?'

'Surely Mr Arora hasn't got a thing for her. She must be at least fifteen years older than he is.' I watched in disbelief as Molly and Kim went into the living room, chatting and laughing, and closed the door firmly behind them.

'Kim and I are going to have words, for sure,' I muttered crossly.

'Oh never mind Kim,' Jazz said with impatience. 'What about Mr Arora?'

'Some men like older women,' said Geena knowledgeably.

'No!' I groaned. 'This is all going horribly wrong.'

'You mean Auntie's going to be miserable, and so, it follows, are we,' said Geena.

'And whose fault is that?' Jazz demanded. 'I told you we should have left Molly Mahal in Reading.'

'Look' – I was glad of any distraction at that point – 'here's Dad.'

Dad was wandering along the street, briefcase in hand, looking lost. He stopped outside Number Ten, opened the gate and made to walk inside. Then he stopped uncertainly, bent to peer at the number on the gatepost and closed the gate again.

'What's the matter with him?' asked Geena.

Dad came closer. Now we could see that his eyes were pink and streaming with tears.

'Dad!' Geena hurried to meet him. 'Are you ill?'

'Is this our house?' Dad asked, squinting wildly.

'Yes, this is it,' I replied, taking his arm. 'Come along, we'll help you inside.'

Jazz was staring at him. 'You look different, Dad.'

'Well, duh,' I said. 'He doesn't usually walk around crying his eyes out.'

'No, something else.' Jazz frowned. 'Where are your glasses?'

'In my pocket.' Dad stepped gingerly through the gate. 'I'm just trying out my new contact lenses.'

'They're not doing a lot for you at the moment, Dad.' I steered him out of the flowerbed. 'Can you see?'

'They were fine until just now,' Dad replied. 'Then I got some dust in my eyes.'

'Here.' Jazz gave him a tissue.

'I hope that's clean,' said Geena severely.

'I've only blown my nose once today,' Jazz retorted.

'I didn't know you were getting contact lenses, Dad,' I remarked.

Dad blinked a few times. He looked sheepish and, strangely, guilty. 'I just thought I'd give them a try,' he mumbled, hurrying towards the open front door almost as if he were trying to avoid awkward questions. As he went in, he almost collided with Molly, who had stepped out of the living room.

'We'd like some tea,' she was calling in an imperious tone to Auntie. Then she stopped and peered up at Dad, who's quite tall and towers over her. 'Where are your glasses? Have you got contact lenses?'

Dad nodded even more sheepishly and began shuffling from foot to foot like a naughty boy.

'What a good idea,' gushed Molly. 'They suit you much better than those boring glasses.' She smiled flirtatiously. 'You look years younger.'

'Oh, thank you,' Dad said, blushing like an idiot.

'Do join us for tea,' Molly said. She cast an impatient glance down the hall at Auntie, who was standing in the kitchen doorway. 'If it ever arrives, that is.'

'I'll see if it's ready,' said Dad quickly, not too blind to notice the look on Auntie's face.

Molly flashed him a gorgeous smile and closed the door again. I wondered what on earth she and Kim could be talking about.

'Johnny,' Auntie began in a dangerous voice, 'you're going to have to do something about that woman. And soon, before there's a murder in this very house.'

'I thought we talked about this last week,' Dad said sternly. 'I don't see any point in discussing it again.' He held up a hand as Auntie opened her mouth again. 'No. And now' – he blinked rapidly several times, eyes watering again – 'I'm going to remove my contact lenses. Excuse me.'

He fumbled his way out of the kitchen, tripping over Geena's foot on the way.

'So that's that,' Auntie muttered savagely. She grabbed the kettle and filled it, clanging it loudly against the sink. The three of us winced. 'I obviously have no say in the matter at all.'

'I hope you're looking forward to this weekend, Amber,' Geena breathed lightly in my ear. 'It's going to be such fun.'

Monday morning came round at the pace of a snail. We grabbed it like a lifeline. Predictably, Auntie had been like a demon all weekend. To avert a major incident, Dad had actually taken Molly shopping on Saturday morning to keep them apart. Three phone calls from Mr Arora pleading the case for the Bollywood party had only added to the tension. Auntie had spent the weekend cooking and baking madly for the party, and we'd been asked to help. Did I say *asked*? Make that *forced*.

Also very predictably, Geena and Jazz blamed

me for Auntie's bad mood. I was in a bad mood myself. Kim was not forthcoming over her secret conversation with Molly Mahal and had all but told me to mind my own business. In an assertive way, of course.

'Free at last,' Jazz sang joyfully, slinging her school bag onto her shoulder. We all turned to wave at Auntie, who was watching us leave, her face pressed wistfully against the living-room window. 'I love school. I so love it.'

'We've got the sponsored walk this Thursday,' I reminded her.

'I don't care,' Jazz replied. 'I'd walk a million miles to get away from Auntie and Molly Mahal at the moment.'

'Girls!' Mrs Dhaliwal was waving at us from the other side of the road. Hitching up her sari, she rushed across to us, scorning the zebra crossing, which was only a few metres away. A guy in a BMW screeched to a halt, narrowly avoiding squashing her. He began yelling. Mrs Dhaliwal ignored him.

'So how's our film star?' she demanded breathlessly.

'Fine,' Geena snapped.

Mrs Dhaliwal winked. She seemed full of excitement about something or other. 'I saw her on Saturday. She was out shopping with your dad.'

'Yes,' I agreed.

Mrs Dhaliwal winked again, several times. I wondered if she had a nervous twitch. 'Well, I won't say any more now,' she said smugly. 'Let's just wait and see what happens, shall we?'

'Yes, let's,' said Geena, looking puzzled.

'This is just what you need, isn't it, girls?' Mrs Dhaliwal crowed. 'Someone to look after you. A new mum. But' – she put her finger to her lips and shushed herself theatrically – 'I'm not going to say another word.'

Beaming, she bounced off down the street.

'What the hell was all that about?' Jazz asked.

Geena was staring at me. Her eyes and mouth were round Os of horror. 'She didn't mean – she *couldn't* mean . . . Not Molly Mahal?'

'And *Dad*?' I gasped.

CHAPTER 6

'Excuse me?' Jazz looked at Geena, then me. 'Molly Mahal and *Dad*? You mean, Dad, our father?'

'How many dads have you got?' I said. I was cold, icy. Actually shivering. It couldn't be true. *It could not be true.*

'But—' Geena began. She stopped, lost for words.

'Mrs Dhaliwal thinks Dad's going to marry Molly Mahal?' Jazz shrieked, as it finally kicked in. 'Is she *mad*?'

'Possibly,' said Geena in a dazed voice.

'What do you mean, *possibly*?' Jazz wailed. 'Dad doesn't want to get married again! He misses Mum too much.'

'Maybe that's exactly why he wants another wife,' I said.

We stared at each other helplessly. We were in shock. Never in our wildest dreams, never, even when we were doing our best to find Auntie a husband, had the idea of Dad wanting to marry again ever occurred to us. It was the worst and most appalling thought that had ever entered our three heads. Now that Mrs Dhaliwal had put it there, it had taken root and was growing at an alarming speed.

'All right' – Geena rallied a bit – 'maybe Dad might want to get married again eventually. But that doesn't mean he's going to marry Molly Mahal.'

'She's a lot older than him,' Jazz said. 'It'd be so – so *dysfunctional*.'

'Have you been watching Jerry Springer again?' demanded Geena.

'Dad seems to like her, though.' I thought back with dread to the times Dad had stood up for Molly against Auntie. 'He doesn't seem bothered about how long she stays with us—'

'He's only being kind,' Geena broke in. 'Or maybe he just wants to show Auntie who's the boss.'

'But he gets all embarrassed when Molly compliments him,' I pointed out.

'Those contact lenses!' Jazz groaned. 'D'you think he's trying to make her fancy him?'

'She does flirt with him,' Geena pointed out.

'She flirts with Mr Arora,' I said quickly. 'She even flirts with Leo. I don't think we can read anything into that.'

'What are we going to *do*?' asked Jazz in despair. 'This can't be happening.' Her bottom lip began to quiver slightly. It made her look about five years old again. 'I don't *want* another mum.'

My eyes began to sting. My throat hurt. I blinked, biting the inside of my mouth ferociously to stop tears.

'We'd better not jump to conclusions,' Geena said gravely. 'If it *isn't* true, we don't want to put any ideas into Dad's head.'

'You're right,' I agreed. 'We'll keep an eye on them and see if we can find out what's going on.'

'Yes,' said Geena. 'Let's watch them for the next few days. Then we can make up our minds whether we have to interfere or not.'

'You three look like you're up to something.'

The voice behind us was totally unexpected. We all shrieked with surprise and leaped into the air. Kim, who had come up behind us unnoticed, also yelled and jumped backwards nervously.

'What are you doing, sneaking up on us like that?' I demanded.

'Sorry.' Kim looked sheepish.

'I thought apologizing wasn't assertive behaviour,' I said, a bit meanly.

'Oh no,' replied Kim earnestly, 'I can apologize when I'm in the wrong.'

We continued walking in silence. I flicked a

warning look at Geena and Jazz, and raised my eyebrows in a meaningful way. I didn't want to discuss Dad and Molly Mahal in front of Kim. She was far too matey with Molly for my liking.

'So what were you talking about?' Kim asked. Her new confidence was becoming quite tiresome. 'You looked very serious.'

'Did we?' I said no more.

'Yes. What's going on?'

Kim was obviously determined to pursue it. I thought fondly of previous times when I could have shut her up with a single look.

'If you tell me what you and Molly Mahal were talking about last week,' I said, 'I'll tell you what *we* were talking about.'

Kim looked agonized. 'I can't,' she said. 'She asked me not to say. Sorry.'

'Oh, you're apologizing,' I said. 'Does that mean you're in the wrong again?'

'No.' Kim looked confused. 'At least, I don't think so.'

'Was it anything to do with our dad?' demanded Jazz.

'No.' Kim looked puzzled. 'Why should it be?' I knew she was telling the truth. She's not that good an actress.

We marched on in silence. I didn't know what Kim was thinking. But I had a good idea of what was on Geena and Jazz's minds. How we could stop Dad from possibly making the biggest mistake of his life. Also, how to stop our own lives from being ruined for evermore.

'I have four blisters,' Jazz moaned. 'One on the big toe of my left foot. One—'

'Do shut up, Jasvinder,' I said, as we limped out of the school building. 'Or I won't be responsible for my actions.'

Thursday. The sponsored walk was over, and we'd finally been allowed to go home. All around us, footsore pupils were trudging, shuffling and limping their way across the playground, cursing Mr Grimwade under their breath. His part in all this had been to stand on the sidelines urging us on to do yet another lap. He reminded me of that guy who shouts encouragement at Roman slaves rowing a war galley. Except, fortunately for us, Mr Grimwade didn't have a whip in his hand.

'Let's get out of here before Kim catches us up,' I said, glancing over my shoulder, 'or we won't get a chance to talk.'

We had been secretly watching Dad and Molly Mahal for the last three days. Geena had suggested that we observe them closely and each of us would draw our own individual conclusions. Then we'd see if all three of us agreed. We'd planned a grand discussion that morning on the way to school but Kim had joined us just after we'd left the house. We hadn't been able to talk.

'I shall never be able to walk fast again,' Geena moaned. 'My toes are deformed.'

'Well done, girls.' At that very moment Mr Arora himself jogged past. He looked as fresh as a daisy, despite having done the sponsored walk alongside us. The sight of him in his shorts had kept many of the girls going round the long, hard course. 'See you later.'

I waved at him. 'See you, sir.'

We left the playground and moved further down the street at pretty much a snail's pace, wincing and complaining.

'Let's get this over with, shall we?' I said. 'Who's going to start?'

'I'm the oldest,' Geena began.

'I'm the youngest,' said Jazz.

'I'm the prettiest,' I added.

'Let's stick to the facts,' Geena scoffed. 'I'll go first.'

'All right then,' Jazz agreed. 'Do you think anything's going on between Dad and Molly?'

Geena frowned. She twirled a lock of hair round her finger while she thought about it. Jazz and I waited patiently. Geena sighed. 'I'm not sure,' she said at last.

'Oh, please!' I snapped. 'After all that.'

'We didn't say we *had* to decide one way or another,' Geena said defensively. 'There's definitely something going on with Dad. But I don't know if it has anything to do with Molly or not.'

'Is that it?' I asked with pointed sarcasm.

'Your turn then,' Geena snapped, looking highly offended.

'He's not interested in her,' I said. 'I'm sure of it—'

'He is,' Jazz broke in defiantly. 'And I've got proof.'

Geena and I stared at her.

'What proof?' I demanded.

'You remember Dad came home with all those shopping bags yesterday?' Jazz said importantly. 'Well, I know what he bought.'

'Don't keep us in suspense,' Geena urged.

'Calvin Klein boxer shorts.' Jazz nodded wisely. 'Now do you see?'

'Dad came home with five bags full of Calvin Klein boxers?' I asked.

'No,' Jazz said impatiently. 'I only had time to look inside one bag. But you know what it means, don't you?'

'Dad needs some new underwear?' I hazarded.

'Yes, but Calvins!' Jazz said pointedly. 'Don't you remember, Mum was always on at him to throw his scruffy old Y-fronts out and buy new ones.'

'So he's finally done it.' Geena shrugged. 'I can't see that it's got much to do with Molly Mahal.'

'Well—' began Jazz.

'Let's not go there,' I said quickly. 'To be honest, I don't think there's anything going on. Dad's nice to her, but he doesn't flirt.'

'Dad can't flirt,' said Jazz. 'It's not in his genes.'

'And anyway' – triumphantly I played my ace – 'Auntie hasn't noticed anything. You know what she's like. If she thought there was anything happening between Dad and Molly, she'd be onto it like a shot.'

'That's true,' began Geena, looking brighter.

'Auntie's too busy with the party to notice what's right under her nose,' Jazz scoffed.

'Yes,' Geena agreed.

'So who do you think is right?' I asked her. 'Me or Jazz?'

'I'm not sure,' muttered Geena.

'Oh, forget it,' I said, disgusted. 'There's a fence. Go sit on it.'

We walked on in silence. Secretly I felt the same way as Geena. I didn't really know what to think. I knew what I *wanted* to think. But that was a different thing altogether.

Jazz cleared her throat. 'I've got a radical idea,'

she said nervously. 'It's the kind of idea Amber might have.'

Geena groaned.

'It must be good then,' I said. 'Spit it out.'

'What if we told Auntie and asked her what *she* thought?' Jazz blurted out. 'Don't hit me.'

'You mean get Auntie's help?' asked Geena.

'That *is* radical,' I remarked.

Jazz looked downcast. 'I told you it was stupid.'

'No,' Geena said. 'It's not. I think it's sensible.'

'If it was *my* idea, you'd say it was rubbish,' I complained. 'Oh, all right. Yes. I think we should do it.'

'Good,' whispered Jazz.

'We'll do it when we get home,' I whispered back. 'Why are we whispering?'

'Look. There. Then tell me I'm wrong.' Jazz pointed ahead, down the street.

Dad and Molly Mahal were standing by our car. They had their heads together, chatting and laughing. They appeared cosy and couple-like.

'Oh, help,' Geena murmured in an agonized voice.

'I told you I was right,' Jazz said. 'But I wish I wasn't.'

'Hello, girls.' I took a little comfort from the fact that Dad didn't look guilty when he saw us. 'How was school?'

'Fine,' I muttered.

'Oh.' Dad looked puzzled. 'I thought you all looked rather depressed.'

'Have you finished work for the day, Dad?' asked Geena.

'No, I just popped home to collect a file I needed.'

Dad did indeed have a blue plastic file under his arm, but I wondered if it was simply an excuse to see Molly.

'Can I give you a lift to the video store?' Dad asked, turning to Molly.

'Certainly not,' Molly replied flirtatiously. She put her hand on Dad's arm. Our eyes widened. 'It's only just round the corner. I wouldn't hear of it. You'd better get straight back to work, you naughty man.'

I thought I could hear Geena grinding her teeth next to me.

'It's only a minute out of my way.' Dad held the passenger door open politely. 'Jump in.'

Smiling, Molly slid gracefully into the front seat. 'Well, thank you,' she purred.

'I thought Auntie usually went to the video store for you,' Jazz remarked coldly.

'Well, Mr Basra gets so excited when I go there myself,' laughed Molly, fluttering her long eye-lashes. 'It seems a shame to let him down.'

Dad waved as they drove off. We stood and watched them turn the corner with heavy hearts.

'We'd better talk to Auntie right away,' Geena said soberly.

We trailed miserably up to the front door. It was difficult to accept the idea that Dad might, some day, marry again. It was even worse to think that he had already found the woman he wanted to marry. But the most awful thing of all was that the woman just might be Molly Mahal.

It wasn't that I didn't like her.

Well . . .

All right.

It was.

Molly, however, didn't make it *easy* to like her. She blew hot and cold; sometimes she was pleasant and sometimes she was moody. You never knew how she was going to be from one minute to the next. You couldn't get close to her because she didn't show enough of her real feelings. And what she did show seemed totally self-obsessed and self-absorbed. I had an uneasy feeling that she always had some other, secret motive for the things she did; that she was only ever thinking of Molly Mahal. I suppose we're all like that in some way. But because she was so into herself, I could no way imagine her as our stepmother; couldn't even begin to imagine talking to her about teenage stuff like boys and bras and periods. I couldn't imagine her as *anyone's* mother.

We let ourselves into the house. As we abandoned bags, coats and trainers in the hall, Auntie came down the stairs.

'Oh!' Jazz shrieked theatrically. 'What *do* you look like?'

'Please excuse her,' Geena said. 'We expected to find our aunt at home, but she seems to have been kidnapped and replaced by a Martian.'

'Very amusing,' said Auntie. She was wrapped in Dad's tatty towelling bathrobe, and her face was coated in a thick, bright-green face-pack. Her wet hair was bundled into a bright-orange towel, and the colour clash was just too much. 'This is the only chance I ever have to get into the bathroom, when Madam Mahal goes to the video store. Now, shall I make you a cup of tea while I wait for my face-pack to harden?'

'We'll do it,' I said instantly. 'You sit down and put your feet up.'

Auntie was stunned – you could see that even under the face-pack. 'What are you three up to now?' she began.

I shrugged. 'Nothing at all. Go on.'

Auntie climbed carefully down the last few steps. She'd painted her toenails and stuck between her toes she had those foam separators

133

that make you walk like a zombie. She tottered into the living room and sat down.

'That wasn't a good idea, Amber,' Jazz grumbled. 'She'll expect us to make tea all the time now.'

'Ssh.' I closed the kitchen door. 'We haven't decided yet how we're going to ask her about Dad.'

'Well,' said Geena, 'I think we should just tell her straight out.'

'Oh, you're volunteering then,' I said, relieved. 'Good.'

'No, I'm not volunteering,' Geena cut in. 'It's embarrassing.'

'You're the oldest,' Jazz reminded her smugly.

'You're the youngest,' retorted Geena. Then looked puzzled.

'Oh, be quiet,' I said. 'I'll do it.'

I made the tea and Geena put some biscuits on a plate. Jazz carried the tray into the living room, where Auntie was relaxing in one of the leather armchairs.

'This is very nice of you, girls,' she said. 'Especially as you've already assured me you have no ulterior motive.'

'Well,' I said, as Jazz put the tray down on the coffee table, 'that's not quite true.'

'Oh?' Auntie enquired suspiciously.

'It's not what you think,' I said, pouring her a cup of tea. 'We just want to talk to you. It's important.'

The doorbell rang.

Auntie jumped, almost spilling her tea. 'Oh, heavens!' she gasped. 'Who can that be?'

'I'll see,' Geena said, heading for the door.

'No!' Auntie hissed frantically. 'Look at the state of me. Find out who it is first.'

Geena peered cautiously through the net curtain. 'Oh!' she gasped. 'It's Mr Arora!'

Auntie clapped a hand to her mouth and covered it in face-pack. 'Don't let him in!' she ordered.

We all stood there in a state of suspended animation. The doorbell rang again.

'Why don't you sneak upstairs?' suggested Jazz. 'We can let him in while you wash that stuff off.'

'Don't,' Geena said urgently, as Auntie made for the door. 'He's looking through the glass.'

'Quick!' whispered Auntie. I think she was pale under all the bright green. 'The back room!'

We dived through the sliding doors that divided the two rooms. Geena slid the doors quietly shut and we stood in a row with our backs against it like suspects in a police line-up.

The doorbell rang insistently.

'What now?' Jazz asked.

'He'll go away if we keep quiet,' said Auntie.

We waited. A few moments passed.

'He must have gone by now,' I whispered.

'No,' said Auntie in a strangled voice. 'I don't think so.'

Mr Arora and Molly Mahal were standing in the back garden, outside the French windows on the other side of the room. They were staring in at us. The looks on their faces told us they thought we were completely insane.

'Oh!' Auntie said in a quivering voice. She headed for the hall, stopping only to remove her foam toe separators. A fatal mistake. It slowed her down just long enough for Molly Mahal to unlock the back door and usher Mr Arora inside.

'What are you all doing hiding in here?' Molly demanded, putting a videotape down on the table. 'Didn't you hear the doorbell? I only just caught Jai as he was about to leave.'

Mr Arora looked acutely uncomfortable. He kept stealing glances at Auntie's bright-green face.

'Molly-ji invited me to tea today,' he mumbled. 'I thought you knew.'

'Obviously I didn't,' Auntie said frostily. 'I prefer to be more formally dressed when we have visitors. Excuse me.' And she swept out of the room, quite regally, considering.

'So that's why he said, "See you later, girls,"' Geena murmured in my ear.

'Wasn't it lucky I took the back-door key with me?' Molly went on, escorting Mr Arora into the living room. 'Or we wouldn't have been able to get in. Ah, tea! Do sit down.'

Mr Arora looked a little wretched. He sat down and accepted a cup of tea, but he was fidgeting and staring at his shoes. Molly, however, didn't seem to care one bit. It wouldn't have surprised me if she hadn't even noticed that Auntie looked like a freak from outer space.

I tapped Geena and Jazz on the shoulders and pointed upstairs. We slipped silently away.

Auntie was in Geena's bedroom. She'd washed the cream off her face and was brushing out her wet hair with long, savage strokes. As we entered, she threw an icy glare in our direction.

'I'm not discussing what just happened,' she warned tightly.

'This isn't about Mr Arora.' I sat down on the bed next to her. Geena and Jazz went to stand by the window. 'It's something else.'

Auntie was still muttering under her breath and only giving me half her mind.

'Do you think Dad's happy?' I asked, plunging straight in.

That got her attention. Auntie looked startled. 'Johnny? Happy?'

'Yes. Do you think Dad's all right?'

'Well . . .' Auntie considered. 'He misses your mum, of course.'

'Do you think he misses being married?' I wanted to know.

'Possibly. All the research shows that men who are married are happier than those who aren't,' Auntie replied. 'I don't know about women though.' She scowled.

'So do you think Dad might want to get married again some day?'

'Oh.' Auntie thought for a moment. 'It's likely. He's still quite young, only in his early thirties. And when you girls leave home for university or whatever, he'll be on his own.'

'You'll be here,' Jazz remarked.

'Well' – Auntie pursed her lips, an enigmatic look on her face – 'I may be here, I may not.'

'Yes, you might get married yourself,' Geena said innocently.

Auntie looked peevish. I hurried to ask my next question.

'But you don't know if Dad's thinking about it at the moment?'

Geena and Jazz were shifting restlessly by the window. I knew they were irritated by my round-about route. But I had been hoping that Auntie, with her usual sharpness, would cut straight through to the heart of the matter and realize what we were worried about. I guess the incident with Mr Arora had left her rattled.

'Oh dear.' Auntie put down her hairbrush and turned to me. 'Is that what you three girls are worrying about? Don't give it another thought. I'm sure your dad isn't ready to re-marry just yet.'

I realized I was going to have to spell it out for her. 'So you don't think he wants to marry Molly Mahal?'

The change in Auntie was quite stupendous. It was like watching a volcano come to life and bubble over. First her jaw dropped. Then her eyes widened. She put her hands up to her face. Her expression was one of sheer horror.

'WHAT!' she shrieked.

I shrugged. 'Mrs Dhaliwal said she thought they might get married.'

'No,' Auntie said through her teeth. It was almost a moan. '*No*. That's absolute rubbish.'

'Oh, good,' I said, relieved. 'So you agree with me and not Jazz.'

'What about the Calvin Klein underwear?' Jazz cut in mutinously.

Auntie swung round. 'Your dad's been buying Calvin Klein underwear?'

'Boxers,' Jazz said knowingly. 'And he hasn't bought any new ones for *ages*.'

Suddenly Auntie looked uncertain. 'I would have noticed if something had been going on,' she muttered, almost to herself. 'But Johnny *has* been different lately. I have noticed that.' She shook her head. 'But it may be that he's just trying to get to grips with his life again. Sort himself out after what happened to your mum.'

At that moment we heard the front door close.

'Mr Arora's gone,' said Jazz. 'He didn't stay long.'

'I think he felt bad about catching you unexpectedly like that,' I told Auntie.

'So he should,' replied Auntie. But her face softened somewhat.

'What *are* we going to do?' Jazz asked impatiently. 'About Dad, I mean.'

'We didn't think it was a good idea to ask Dad about Molly straight out,' added Geena. 'We didn't want to put ideas in his head.'

'You're right there,' Auntie agreed. 'But there *is* something we can do.' She yanked off her dressing gown and began to dress. 'We can try to get rid of Molly before things get too serious.'

'How?' we three said together.

'Leave it to me.' Auntie swept over to the door. 'Come along.'

We followed her downstairs. Molly was sitting straight-backed on the sofa, finishing a cup of Darjeeling tea and a ginger biscuit. She'd put on a bit of weight over the last ten days, and her new curves suited her. She didn't offer us either tea or biscuits. I don't think she was being rude; I think it just never crossed her mind to consider anyone else.

Auntie collected the local newspaper from the magazine rack and sat down on the sofa. We followed her example. We were dying to see what she was going to do.

'Molly-ji, we have to talk,' Auntie said briskly.

'Oh?' A wary look flashed across Molly's face, reminding me of a hunted animal. 'Do we?'

'Well, obviously you're very welcome here' – Auntie managed to get the words out without choking, even with a semblance of warmth – 'but we must start thinking about what's going to happen when you leave.'

Molly didn't answer. She simply sat there gazing at Auntie, her eyebrows delicately arched in query.

'So I thought it was time you found a job.' Auntie opened the newspaper at the Jobs Vacant section. She spread it out flat on the coffee table.

'A job?' Molly Mahal sounded as if Auntie had offered to take her outside and garrotte her.

'Yes. Now, let's see what's available.' Auntie scanned the newspaper. 'What qualifications do you have?'

Geena and Jazz nudged me. I knew what they were thinking. Auntie was onto a loser before she had even started.

'I'm very good at dancing,' Molly replied dryly. 'Oh, and I can mime to playback songs.'

'Not much call for those skills, I'm afraid.' Auntie didn't miss a beat. 'It says here that McDonald's are looking for staff.'

'I'm a vegetarian,' Molly said quickly. 'And the uniform wouldn't suit me.'

'Here's one,' Auntie went on, undaunted. 'Receptionist for upmarket hotel required. No previous experience necessary. Must be willing to work hard . . .' Her voice tailed away.

Molly stood up. 'I made my first film when I was eighteen years old,' she said in a clear voice. 'I've never had another job.'

Auntie held out the newspaper. 'Well, you ought to think about it at least,' she said, quite gently.

'It seems that I only have two choices,' Molly snapped, her nose in the air. 'One, I return to the movies. Or two, I get married.'

She turned and walked out of the room, leaving us all in a flutter.

CHAPTER 7

'See?' Jazz sat up in bed and poked me. 'I knew I was right.'

'If you don't stop saying that, you'll be oh so sorry.' I pushed my hair out of my eyes and glared at her.

'Well, I *am* right,' Jazz insisted. 'I mean, Molly's not going to get back into the movies, is she? You heard her yourself. Her only other option is to get married— Urrgh!'

I'd just thumped her very satisfyingly round the head with my pillow. 'Will you shut up? It doesn't mean she's going to marry *Dad*.'

'What else does it mean?' Jazz spluttered. I didn't answer. I simply began rolling her up in the duvet like a hot dog.

'Girls, time to get up.' Auntie poked her head round the door. She looked as if she hadn't slept very well either. There were black rings round her eyes, and her hair was a bird's nest.

After Molly's worrying statement the day

before, we'd had a council of war. Auntie had decided that she was going to try and talk to Dad at the weekend. Until then, we'd just have to wait and see what happened.

Jazz was now rolled up tightly in the middle of the duvet, her head sticking out of one end and her feet out of the other. I sat on the edge of the duvet so she couldn't escape.

'It's Friday,' I reminded Auntie. 'There's another meeting at school about the party. You *are* coming, aren't you?'

Auntie looked diffident. 'I'm not sure,' she mumbled.

'Oh, nonsense,' I said bracingly. 'You don't want Mr Arora to think you're embarrassed about yesterday, do you?'

'Well, of course she's embarrassed,' Jazz cut in, trying to free herself. 'She was standing in front of him with a bright-green face. It doesn't get any more embarrassing than that.'

'Thank you, Jasvinder,' said Auntie. 'I'm grateful you spelled that out for me.'

'We'll see you there,' I said with bright encouragement. 'And we'll wait for you outside. So you don't have to go in on your own.'

Auntie sighed and left.

'Can you please unroll me now?' Jazz demanded.

I grabbed the edge of the duvet and shook it.

Jazz tumbled out and landed on the floor with a shriek.

Geena came in. 'Ssh,' she said. 'Our future step-mother's still in bed.'

'Don't joke,' I snapped. 'It's not funny.'

'I thought humour was a good tension-reliever,' Geena remarked.

'Well, it's adding to *my* tension,' I muttered. I felt more responsible for the situation than the others. Of course I did. It had been my idea to invite Molly Mahal to stay. It had back-fired horribly.

I slipped out of the bedroom and went along the landing to the bathroom. The door was ajar. I could hear the radio. A breathy female voice was singing a sweet love-song that had been in the charts for the last few weeks, and Dad was whistling merrily along.

I stopped and looked in. He was standing in front of the mirror, a Santa Claus beard of white shaving foam on his face. I realized with a jolt how well he looked now. He'd been gaunt and thin, hollow-cheeked, after Mum. Now he looked fit and relaxed again. Was it because of Molly Mahal?

As all these thoughts passed through my mind, Dad caught my eye in the mirror. 'Morning, Amber,' he said cheerfully. 'I won't be a minute.'

'All right, Dad.'

I had a lump as big as a football in my throat. As I waited on the landing, I wondered what I'd done. We'd just had to cope with all the upheaval of Auntie moving in and turning our lives upside down. Surely the same thing couldn't, wouldn't happen all over again.

'No, don't go in yet.' I stopped Geena from pulling open the glass doors which led into the upper school. 'I told Auntie we'd wait for her out here so that we can go into the meeting together.'

'I guess she does need some moral support,' Geena agreed. 'I mean, she did make an almighty fool of herself in front of the guy she fancies to bits.'

'I think she knows that,' I replied.

'Hasn't today been awful?' Jazz complained, kicking at a Coke can which was rolling its way across the vast, landscaped expanse of the upper school playground. 'I haven't been able to stop thinking about Dad and Molly Mahal. Miss Véronique went mad at me because I got my French verbs all wrong.'

'You hate French,' Geena pointed out. 'You always get your verbs wrong.'

'Well' – Jazz looked aggrieved – 'at least I've got a *reason* this time.'

'Mr Arora could hardly look me in the eye this

morning,' I remarked. 'I think he feels really bad about yesterday, although he didn't say anything.'

'Look,' remarked Geena, 'here's Kim.'

Kim was looking as full of the joys of spring as Dad. She bounded over the crossing, waving cheerily at a lorry driver who stopped for her. Her face changed when she saw us, though. You could almost say it dropped.

'Hello,' she said in an almost normal voice. 'It's nearly time for the meeting to start, isn't it?'

'We're waiting for Auntie,' I explained.

'Oh.' Kim frowned. She looked worried. Why, I didn't have a clue.

'Don't let us keep you,' Jazz said kindly. 'You go in if you want to.'

'No,' replied Kim, too quickly. 'I'll wait with you.'

'Seen Molly recently?' I asked.

'Seen her?' Kim looked flustered. 'No. Not *seen* her.'

There was something going on. In another moment the new assertive Kim would be having one of her old panic attacks. I wondered if she really did know anything about Molly's intentions towards Dad, and if that was the reason why she was blushing and shuffling her feet and looking agonized.

I was deciding whether to quiz Kim there and

then, when Auntie's VW turned into the car park.

'Oh, here she is.' Kim looked utterly relieved. 'I'll see you inside. I've just remembered, I left my science homework behind.'

Without another word she shot off, crossed the road again and disappeared back into the lower school playground.

Geena shrugged. 'The strain of being permanently assertive must have turned her brain,' she remarked. 'What's the matter with the girl?'

'There's something going on,' I said with grim certainty. 'And I, for one, intend to find out what it is.'

'Thank you for waiting, girls,' Auntie said as she joined us. She looked pretty in a stylish black trouser suit and white shirt, but she seemed nervous. 'Let's get this over with.'

The 'volunteers' were milling around in the hall, waiting for Mr Grimwade to show. There was a buzz of excited chatter. A rumour was going round that Mr Morgan had been called before the local education authority to explain his 'budget', and everyone was talking about it.

Mr Arora was on the watch for us. As soon as we entered the hall, he rushed towards us. His face was pink and his tie was askew. He seemed very embarrassed.

'Oh, hello,' he said breathlessly to Auntie. 'Thank you for coming. I was hoping you would.'

'Did you think I wouldn't?' Auntie enquired coolly.

'No. Yes.' Mr Arora looked quite wretched. 'Er – I'm sorry about yesterday.'

We all looked expectantly at Auntie.

She shrugged. 'Forget it,' she said.

'Well. Thank you.' Mr Arora seemed more embarrassed, not less. 'You – er – look very nice today.'

'Better than yesterday, you mean?' said Auntie. 'That's not difficult.' But she smiled. Mr Arora smiled too. We all smiled.

We could quite possibly have stood there smiling for some time. At that moment, though, Mr Grimwade appeared, looking rather bad-tempered.

'Sir,' said Jack Freeman, a rather stupid boy who's in Geena's year, 'is it true that Mr Morgan's going to prison for spending all the school's money?'

'Don't be ridiculous, boy,' boomed Mr Grimwade. 'The school has plenty of money. Plenty, 1 say.'

'There's at least five pounds in the teachers' biscuit fund,' offered Mr Hernandez.

Mr Grimwade glared at him and made a great show of bustling to his seat. Everybody did likewise.

'Shall we sit together?' Mr Arora took Auntie's arm. 'There are some details I need to discuss with you.'

I looked sideways at Geena and Jazz. It seemed as if the romance between Auntie and Mr Arora was back on track. Just at that very millisecond they were hovering on the brink of a new understanding, a new relationship, perhaps even a new future.

This was before Molly Mahal walked in.

The door was flung open. Molly swept into the hall, a stunning vision in an aquamarine lengha stitched with gold. At the moment she appeared, the sun finally burst out from behind the grey clouds, where it had been hiding all day, and sent a brilliant shaft of light through the huge glass windows. It lit Molly Mahal with a radiant sunburst so that she glittered and shone all over.

Everyone was struck dumb. Always one with an eye to the main chance, Molly paused in the doorway. Then she nodded regally at the assembled throng, and moved gracefully towards Mr Arora. I noticed Kim behind her.

'It's Molly,' Jazz spluttered, somewhat unnecessarily.

'Good afternoon,' Molly said graciously, holding out her hand to Mr Arora. Beside him Auntie had turned to stone like a character in a fairy tale. 'I hope I'm not interrupting anything.'

'No, no, no.' At first, Mr Arora seemed incapable of stringing a sentence together. Then he rallied. 'We're very pleased to see you.' He turned to Mr Grimwade, who was goggle-eyed, along with the rest of us. '*This* is Molly Mahal.'

There was a sharp intake of breath which visibly gratified Molly.

'What *is* she doing here?' whispered Geena.

'I have no idea,' I replied. 'But I think we're about to find out.'

I had the strangest feeling that we were all extras in a movie, directed by and starring Molly Mahal. So far, she hadn't told the rest of us what the plot was all about. She was the only one who knew.

'Miss Mahal . . .' Mr Grimwade took her hand and held it for about a minute longer than was necessary. 'A great honour.'

'Thank you,' Molly said graciously. She smiled dazzlingly. 'I'm sorry it's taken me so long to make up my mind. But now I'm here to tell you that' – she paused for theatrical effect – 'I would *so* love to be the guest of honour at your party.'

There was a gasp of delight, followed by a ripple of applause. I stared at Molly, wondering why she'd reached this decision all of a sudden. Maybe she'd always intended to do it and had just enjoyed keeping everyone hanging on and being the centre of attention. Or maybe it was part of some other great plan. As ever with her, it was hard to know.

There was a big fat fuss going on now. Mr Arora had abandoned Auntie to find a 'suitable' chair for Molly Mahal, and had left the hall in a great rush. Mr Hernandez gave up the cushion he'd brought along for his bad back to Molly. Everyone crowded round her introducing themselves. Meanwhile Auntie stood to one side, looking – well, poleaxed, I think would just about describe it.

'What's Molly up to?' I whispered to Geena and Jazz. 'Why's she doing this?'

'Who knows?' Geena shrugged. 'One thing's for sure. I don't suppose she's doing it out of the goodness of her heart. There'll be another motive in there somewhere.'

'Well, of course there is,' Jazz said in an exasperated voice. 'Don't you see? She's doing it to impress *Dad*.'

That actually did sound horribly plausible.

'And what's Kim's role in all of this?' Geena demanded.

'That's precisely what I'm going to ask her,' I replied. But I thought I already knew.

I dodged my way round the crowd towards Kim. She saw me coming and made a determined effort to melt into the excited throng around Molly

Mahal. But I cut off her escape route with some swift footwork.

'Hello, Amber,' she said. But assertively speaking, it was a very weak attempt.

'All right,' I said, 'I'll save your blushes. You've been Molly Mahal's spy in the camp, haven't you?'

'I don't know what you mean,' Kim began. 'Well. Yes. I suppose you could look at it that way.'

'Is there another way to look at it?'

'No,' Kim mumbled.

'That's why you volunteered to help with the party, wasn't it?' I went on ruthlessly. 'So you could tell her exactly what was going on.'

Kim gave me a hangdog look. 'She asked me to. I'm sorry, Amber.'

'And what else has she got you doing, Secret Agent Henderson?' I asked.

'Nothing,' Kim said earnestly. 'Really. I just felt sorry for her. I wanted to help her . . .' Her voice tailed away.

'I know,' I said, taking pity on her. 'How do you think I got us into this mess in the first place?'

I returned to Geena and Jazz. 'Kim's been keeping her up to date with all the party details,' I told them. 'Molly must have been planning this.'

'Of course she has,' Geena remarked. 'She could have got a lift here with Auntie, couldn't she? She didn't. She wanted to make a big entrance.'

'She's so melodramatic,' Jazz complained, rather enviously, I thought.

Mr Arora hurried in, dragging an armchair. He must have brought it down from the staff room on the second floor because he was sweating and panting like a marathon runner. He placed it reverently within the circle of plastic chairs, which were deemed suitable for those of us who didn't have film-star bottoms, and led Molly Mahal over to it. Mr Hernandez's cushion was settled ceremoniously at her back, and at last we were ready to begin.

'Well!' Mr Grimwade shuffled his papers and blinked with excitement. 'Firstly, can I say how thrilled we are that Miss Mahal has agreed to be our guest.'

People actually started cheering. Auntie, who had somehow ended up sitting between Jazz and Geena instead of next to Mr Arora, folded her hands tightly in her lap. I wondered how it was all going to end. In tears, probably. I had a feeling it wouldn't be Molly Mahal crying.

'Hear, hear,' said Mr Arora robustly. 'I'm sure we'll sell many more tickets when everyone hears the wonderful news.'

'Oh, yes.' Mr Grimwade rubbed his hands, Scrooge-like, thinking about all those lovely profits.

'Haven't the posters already been done?' Auntie enquired coldly.

'They haven't been photocopied yet,' Mr Arora retorted. 'They can easily be amended.'

Auntie lapsed into a silence one might almost call sulky.

'So perhaps one of you could give us an update on the preparations?' Mr Grimwade asked with a cheerful smile, looking from grim-faced Auntie to defiant Mr Arora.

'Hasn't Grimwade realized that there's something going on yet?' Geena whispered. 'All this raw emotion seething around the hall, right in front of him. He'd have to be blind not to notice.'

'I don't think he's the sensitive type,' I said.

But Mr Grimwade had finally begun to pick up on some sort of atmosphere. Looking puzzled, he turned to Mr Arora and raised his eyebrows.

'Well, a group of the student volunteers have been co-ordinating the making and collection of decorations for the hall,' Mr Arora began. 'And Chapati MC has agreed to do a set for half his normal fee. We've also booked Mr Sagoo's bhangra group to perform.'

'I hope we don't have to pay *them*,' Mr Grimwade interposed sternly.

'Amit says they'll do it for free,' said Miss Patel.

'Excellent.' Mr Grimwade looked considerably brighter.

'We'll put the posters up at the beginning of next week, once we've added the great news.' Mr Arora bowed gallantly in Molly Mahal's direction. 'I'm sure there'll be a mad rush for tickets.'

'Thank you, Mr Arora.' Mr Grimwade turned to Auntie, looking a little nervous. 'And – er – the catering preparations, Miss Dhillon? Are they under control?'

'Of course,' said Auntie quietly. 'The canteen staff have put a freezer at our disposal, and we're filling it at a great rate. The parents have been very good about making food and sending it in with the children.'

'How many people are we expecting, anyway?' Miss Patel asked. 'We don't want to run out of food.'

'Or alcohol,' Mr Hernandez added.

'It will be strictly soft drinks only,' Mr Grimwade said pompously. Mr Hernandez looked depressed.

'We're calculating on selling around a hundred tickets maximum,' Auntie explained. 'I really don't think there'll be a problem with the food running out.'

'How many people can we fit into this hall?'

Until now Molly Mahal had said nothing. She'd simply reclined in her chair, her chin resting on

one slender hand, listening and looking beautiful.
Now she leaned forward and gazed enquiringly
at Mr Grimwade.

'Well . . .' Mr Grimwade considered. 'With fire
regulations and so on . . . About five hundred.'

Molly smiled. 'Then that's the amount we
should be catering for,' she said.

'*Five hundred people?*' Auntie repeated incredulously.

'Oh dear,' whispered Geena. 'Trouble's on its
way.'

'Yes, indeed,' I replied.

'Well, I'm sure there are many people who are
going to turn up to see such a distinguished guest
of honour,' Mr Arora began doubtfully. 'But still,
five hundred! We've never had a school event
that's been even half as well supported as that.'

'You will this time,' Molly said confidently.
'Trust me.'

I looked round at the assembled volunteers. All
were staring at Molly Mahal as if she were the
Holy Grail, the Promised Land, the pot of gold at
the end of the rainbow. They believed in her
utterly.

'You see,' Molly went on breezily, 'it's all down
to publicity. As a movie star, I know about such
things. Leave it to me.' She flashed us a wide, confident smile. 'I'm going to make sure that

everyone – *everyone* – knows about the party at Copperwood School.'

'Coppergate,' I muttered.

'Whatever,' said Molly.

CHAPTER 8

'What do you think she'll do?' asked Jazz. I could see her face in the dressing-table mirror as she brushed her hair. She looked concerned.

'Who knows?' I curled up under the duvet. 'What do film stars usually do that gets them all over the newspapers?'

'They wear clothes which hardly cover them,' Jazz suggested. 'They write books. They get married— Oh!' She clapped a hand to her mouth.

'Relax,' I said. 'I don't think Molly Mahal is going to marry Dad just to publicize the party.'

'I bet she's planning something big though,' Jazz muttered darkly. 'Just to impress him.'

I did not reply. I was becoming ever more concerned that Jazz's assessment of the situation was the right one. I did not want to admit it, however. I *wouldn't* admit it.

The door opened suddenly, and Geena peered in. 'Quick!' she whispered urgently. 'Come downstairs. You have to hear this.'

'Oh, go away.' I pulled my pillow over my head. 'It's Saturday morning. I'm not getting up yet.'

Geena performed a dance of impatience in the doorway. 'Auntie and Dad are in the living room. Talking about Molly.'

'Oh, really.' I stroked my chin. 'Now, let me see. What about the whole question of sneaking around listening to people's private conversations?'

'Sometimes, Amber, you can be so irritating,' Geena retorted, turning on her heel.

'Wait for me.' Jazz threw down her hairbrush and scrambled across the bed towards the door, almost breaking my kneecaps.

I threw back the duvet and followed them out. We could hear Molly splashing around in the bathroom, singing a song from one of her films. Once she was in there, you never knew quite when she was coming out again. Auntie had clearly decided that it was safe to go ahead and talk to Dad.

I tiptoed down the stairs on bare feet. Geena and Jazz were already standing outside the living-room door. They put their fingers to their lips and made exaggerated gestures at me to keep quiet.

'I'm not making any noise, am I?' I demanded, very quietly. Unfortunately for me, my foot slipped on the last step and I plunked down on my bottom with a *thud*. Geena and Jazz both rolled their eyes, but behind the closed door, Dad and Auntie were too busy arguing to take any notice.

'Johnny, I'm not trying to interfere,' Auntie was saying in a would-be reasonable tone, just tinged with irritation. 'I was just wondering if you had any plans to get married again sometime – anytime. That's all.'

'But why are you asking?' demanded Dad. Now, he definitely *did* sound irritated. 'There must be a reason.'

'Not really,' Auntie muttered.

'Oh, don't be a wuss,' breathed Geena. 'Get in there.'

'Well, to be honest . . .' Auntie had decided to go for it. 'We – I – was wondering about Molly.'

'Molly!' Dad repeated. 'You mean, Molly and *me*?'

I pressed my ear against the door, trying to analyse his voice. He sounded shocked and incredulous – yes, but there was something else. What was it? Embarrassment? Annoyance? Relief?

'This is ridiculous,' Dad snapped, sounding quite angry now. 'Am I going to be married off to every female I ever come into contact with? I think we ought to drop this subject right now, before one of us says something we may regret.'

'He's coming!' Geena gasped. 'Quick!'

Callously elbowing Jazz and me out of the way,

she fled up the stairs. Jazz whisked round the corner into the kitchen. Meanwhile, my indecision meant that I only got halfway up the stairs after Geena. With great cunning, I turned round and pretended to be just walking down.

'Oh, morning,' I said with an artificial yawn, as Dad and Auntie stomped out of the living room. Both were red-faced. 'What's for breakfast, Auntie?'

'Nothing for me,' said Dad shortly. He gave Auntie a defiant look. 'Molly's asked me to give her a lift to the shops, and she wants to leave early.'

Auntie shrugged and stalked off to the kitchen, almost colliding with Jazz, who had just walked out, too casually. Dad stomped off upstairs, passing Geena, who was on her way down. She and Jazz hustled me into the living room none too gently.

'See?' Jazz said triumphantly. 'I told you I was right.'

'I'm so sorry.' I raised my eyebrows. 'You'll have to explain. Right about what, exactly?'

Jazz elbowed me in the ribs. 'Dad and Molly, of course.'

'He denied it,' I parried swiftly.

'He didn't, actually,' Geena broke in. 'He said it was ridiculous. But he didn't deny it.'

'And he sounded dead embarrassed, too,' Jazz went on. 'You must have noticed that, Amber.'

'*I* did,' added Geena.

'Since when have *you* started believing all this about Dad and Molly?' I turned on Geena. 'A few days ago you couldn't decide one way or the other.'

'Since we heard him arguing with Auntie just now,' Geena snapped.

'That's the thing about listening to other people's private conversations,' said Auntie, who was standing in the doorway. 'You learn so many interesting things.'

There was nothing to do but squirm and blush and look guilty.

'We didn't hear all of it,' Jazz offered. 'Geena heard more than Amber and I did.'

'Thank you,' Geena said bitterly.

'What did *you* think, Auntie?' I asked with curiosity.

'I think we ought to do what your Dad wants, and drop the subject,' replied Auntie. 'I don't believe he feels that way about Molly at all.' But her tone didn't carry the conviction I was looking and hoping for.

'Of course,' said Jazz later that morning, 'this is all your fault, Amber.'

We were lying on our bed, flicking through some of Auntie's glossy magazines. Downstairs, Auntie was banging around in the kitchen, making another hundred samosas to feed the extra guests Molly Mahal was planning to lure to the party. For once, Auntie hadn't asked us to help. I think she was perfecting her martyr complex.

'Yes,' Geena joined in. 'When she and Dad get married, Amber, you'll only have yourself to blame.'

'They won't get married,' I said with irritation. 'Not now. Not ever. Not even in a parallel universe.'

Jazz began to giggle. 'Auntie must be getting desperate.' She pointed at a page of the magazine she was reading. 'Look at this.'

The back pages of the magazine were filled with advertisements for health spas, jewellery, make-up and cosmetic surgery. ENHANCE YOUR NATURAL ASSETS WITH BREAST IMPLANTS! BOTOX FOR BEGINNERS – MAGIC THOSE UNWANTED WRINKLES AWAY. LOOK YEARS YOUNGER AND LET THE REAL, RADIANT YOU SHINE THROUGH WITH OUR ACID SKIN PEELS. These three advertisements had been ringed with blue pen.

'She must be crazy.' I grinned. 'Do you think they peel your skin off in one big piece from your forehead to your neck?'

Geena was looking a bit sick, I noticed. 'I don't

think it was Auntie,' she said. 'Molly was looking at these magazines yesterday.'

'Molly!' Jazz stopped laughing. 'She must be going all-out to get Dad.'

She and Geena stared accusingly at me.

'What?' I demanded.

'Well, isn't it about time you had one of your daft ideas?' asked Jazz. 'You know, to get us out of this mess?'

'If my ideas are so daft,' I retorted, 'why are you asking?' I did not want to have to admit that, for once, my boundless capacity for problem-solving had deserted me.

'Because you got us *into* this,' snapped Geena.

We sat there glaring at each other. I think we would have eventually come to blows, except that Dad called us from downstairs.

'Let this be a lesson to you, Jazz,' Geena said as we clattered down the stairs. 'These are the consequences of not taking responsibility for one's actions.'

'Will you be quiet?' I muttered.

Auntie, Molly and Dad were in the living room. As we walked in, Dad whipped open his leather jacket, a bit like a male stripper, which was disconcerting to say the very least. 'What do you think, girls?'

He wore a white T-shirt with a huge colour

picture of Molly Mahal's face printed on the front. I think it was a still from *Amir Ladka, Garib Ladka*. Underneath it read: MEET BOLLYWOOD LEGEND MOLLY MAHAL AT COPPERGATE SCHOOL'S END OF TERM PARTY! followed by the date and time. Then it was repeated in Punjabi, Hindi, Gujerati and Bengali.

'Isn't it great?' Dad went on, glancing nervously at Auntie. 'It was Molly's idea.'

'This is just the start,' Molly laughed. She dipped into a plastic bag and pulled out a handful of T-shirts. 'I got some made up for you too, girls.'

'Oh, thank you,' Geena said faintly.

'Put them on, girls.' Auntie was keeping a straight face, but only just. 'Let's see how they look.'

Glumly we pulled the T-shirts on over our clothes. Geena's was too small, mine was too big and Jazz could hardly get her head through hers.

'Lovely,' said Molly Mahal with satisfaction.

'How did you pay for all this?' Auntie asked a little suspiciously. I'd been wondering that too. Surely Dad hadn't footed the bill?

'We went to see Mr Pandit at the print shop,' Dad explained quickly. 'Molly was wonderful. She persuaded him to supply the T-shirts free of charge in return for advertising.'

I looked at the bold, red letters on Jazz's back.

'PANDIT'S PRINT SHOP,' I read out. 'LET ME BE YOUR PRINTS CHARMING!'

'How stylish,' Jazz said grumpily.

'I think it's a fabulous idea,' remarked Auntie, with a faint smirk. 'You can wear them when we go out shopping later, girls.'

'We got one for you too.' Molly handed another T-shirt to Auntie, which wiped the smile off her face ever so quickly. 'I hope it's big enough.'

'We can *all* wear them when we go shopping, Auntie,' Geena said with a grin. Auntie scowled.

'Now I have a phone call to make,' Molly said, batting her eyelashes at Dad. 'So if you'll excuse me . . .' She waved a gently dismissive hand.

'Of course,' Dad said politely. 'Come along, girls.'

We trooped sulkily out, still wearing our T-shirts. Molly accompanied us to the door, and then closed it firmly behind us. I wondered who she was calling.

'Well!' said Auntie, holding up her T-shirt with a look that said it all.

'Get me out,' Jazz wailed, trying to pull the T-shirt over her head. 'I'm stuck.'

Geena and I extracted her.

'I think it's a brilliant idea,' Dad said firmly. 'In fact, I'm going to wear mine to the gym.'

'THE GYM?' we roared in unison.

Dad tried not to blush, but couldn't. 'Yes, the gym,' he said in a would-be casual voice. 'Why not?'

'Dad, you don't do exercise,' I said.

'You take the car to Mr Attwal's shop and it's only a two-minute walk,' added Jazz.

'Then it's time I got fit,' Dad replied, now a fiery red. He couldn't look any of us in the eye. 'I'm going to get my sports kit and go to the gym. I'll be back for lunch. Excuse me.'

We watched him march upstairs.

'You see?' Jazz began.

'Don't start!' I snapped.

Auntie simply looked despairing, and disappeared into the kitchen.

'I told you so.' Jazz glared at me, and Geena joined in. 'Dad and Molly Mahal. It's happening, Amber, whether you like it or not.'

CHAPTER 9

By Monday morning we had a poster advertising the party in our living-room window. Molly Mahal had spent most of the weekend on the telephone. Several of the calls had been to Mr Arora, urging him to hurry finishing the posters. Other calls had been so mysterious that no one else was allowed to hear them. Jazz had tried putting a glass to the living-room wall as they do in the movies, but Auntie had stopped her. We later caught her trying the same trick herself.

'I wonder what else Molly has planned,' Geena said thoughtfully, as we left for school.

'Isn't this enough?' I waved my hand at the poster in our front window.

'Obviously not,' Jazz smirked, looking over my shoulder.

Leo was leaning his bicycle against our hedge. He was wearing a Molly Mahal T-shirt under his denim jacket.

'All right?' He pulled Dad's newspaper out of

his bag and walked up our path. 'Hey, where are your T-shirts?'

'They're not part of our regulation school uniform,' I said frostily, sweeping past him with my nose in the air. Jazz and Geena followed, giggling.

'Good morning, girls.' Mrs Macey was on her way back from the minimarket, clutching a bottle of milk. She too was wearing a Molly T-shirt. It did not sit well with her tweed skirt and sensible shoes. I ground my teeth.

'Well, it's for the school, I suppose,' Geena remarked.

'Everybody's going Molly Mahal crazy,' Jazz moaned. 'Including Dad.'

'Don't look left,' I ordered as we passed the minimarket. 'Eyes straight ahead.'

Mr Attwal had jumped off his stool and was banging on the window, pointing with delight at the Molly T-shirt he was wearing. There was a poster advertising the party taped to the shop door. There were more posters, one pinned to every tree the length of the street.

'I feel like Molly's watching us everywhere we go,' complained Jazz, as we took the short cut through the park. There were posters here too. One on the community notice board, one on the ice-cream stall and one in the children's playground.

When we arrived at school, there was more

stress awaiting us. The first person we met in the school playground was George Botley, bare-chested, with his shirt tied around his waist.

'George, do you want me to be ill?' I asked. 'Put your shirt on immediately.'

George grinned. 'Am I driving you wild?'

'Not so you'd notice,' I replied.

George looked disappointed. Instead of his shirt, he pulled on the T-shirt he'd been holding scrunched up in his hand.

'Molly Mahal!' I groaned. I jumped forward and clutched George round the neck by a handful of material. 'Where did you get that?'

George looked quite pleased, probably because it's the closest I've ever got to him. 'Mr Grimwade and Mr Arora are giving them out,' he said. 'They said we can wear them every day until the party.'

I released him and turned to Geena and Jazz. 'We have to check this out,' I said sternly.

The double doors to one of the Year 7 classrooms were open onto the playground. Mr Arora and Mr Grimwade were standing behind a table holding three huge cardboard boxes. Students were milling around them, and they were handing out Molly T-shirts as fast as they could. Both teachers wore T-shirts themselves, Mr Grimwade's stretched so tight across his bulging stomach it looked as if the baby was due any minute.

'Form an orderly queue now!' Mr Grimwade shouted, but there was no chance of that. Molly Mahal fever had really taken a grip.

'Girls!' Mr Arora spotted us and waved. 'Isn't this great? And we have a queue for tickets at the school office already!' He squinted at us through the morning sunshine. 'Where are your T-shirts?'

'We left them at home,' I called back.

'Thank the Lord,' Geena muttered.

Mr Arora plunged his hands into a box and pulled out a handful of T-shirts. 'Here you are,' he said encouragingly. 'We can lend you some to wear today.'

'Retreat,' Geena said in my ear. 'Now. Before it's too late.'

We began backing away round the side of the school. Luckily a rush of T-shirt seekers swamped Mr Arora at just that moment, shielding us from view.

'This is awful,' Jazz said in a tragic tone. 'It's all to impress Dad, and it's just going so brilliantly.'

Geena and I did not even have the heart to argue.

The school office was still locked, but there was already a queue of ten people at the outside door. Mrs Dhaliwal was one of them. She was having a heated argument with the woman in the blue shalwar kameez who was standing behind her.

'Don't try and push in front of me again,' Mrs

Dhaliwal snapped fearsomely. 'I've been waiting here for twenty minutes, and I'm not in the mood to be trifled with.'

'Is everything all right, Auntie-ji?' Geena asked diplomatically.

'Oh, yes.' Mrs Dhaliwal directed a final glare at the woman behind her. 'Don't mind her. She's just my sister-in-law. Now, how's Molly? And your father?' She gave us a huge wink. 'Everything going well?'

We were saved from answering by the sound of the office door being unlocked by the secretary. We just caught a glimpse of Mrs Capstick's scared face as the queue surged forward.

'This is madness,' Geena said.

'Hello,' said a bright voice behind us.

There was Kim, beaming at us. Of course, she was also wearing a Molly T-shirt.

'Oh!' Kim looked disappointed. 'Why aren't you wearing your T-shirts?'

'How many times do you think we'll be asked that,' I said to Geena and Jazz, 'before we're compelled to kill somebody?'

'Not long.' Jazz eyed Kim irritably. 'My fingers are itching already.'

'I thought you'd be pleased,' Kim grumbled. 'I mean, it's all for the school, isn't it?'

We stared hard at her, but Kim looked very innocent.

'I suppose you'd know if Molly's got any other publicity stunts planned,' I remarked.

This time Kim did turn red. It was as if all the blood in her body rushed to her face at once. 'I might,' she said, attempting a casual tone. She slung her bulging bag off her shoulder and lowered it to the ground in an effort to hide her crimson face. 'I might not.'

'Oh, stop it.' I folded my arms. 'You *do* know.'

'Tell,' demanded Jazz. 'It will save you from much pain.'

'I can't,' Kim said assertively. 'I promised.'

'You *promised*,' I repeated with scorn. 'Kim, how long have we been friends?'

'Seven years,' Kim mumbled.

'And do you remember why we *became* friends?' I pressured her.

'You stopped George Botley from painting my face blue when we were five,' said Kim.

'Yes,' I said sternly. 'But we also became friends because we like and trust each other. Because we respect each other.'

'Oh, please,' Geena said in my ear. 'You'll have us in tears in a minute.'

'Now, are you going to tell us or not?' I asked.

'No,' replied Kim. 'I would if I could, but I can't.'

'Well,' said Geena, who was staring down at Kim's bag lying at her feet. 'Are you going to tell us why you've got a copy of *Masala Express* in your rucksack?'

Kim's eyes widened in horror. We all looked down at her bag. It was so full, bits of things were sticking up out of the sides. A pencil case. A science textbook. A copy of *Masala Express*.

'What in heaven's name are *you* doing with a copy of *Masala Express*?' I asked in amazement.

'Nothing,' Kim mumbled, looking guiltier than the most guilty person in the whole world, ever. She made a dive for her bag, but Geena was quicker. She grabbed at the copy of *Masala Express* and caught the end of it. She then hung on for grim death as Kim tried to pull the bag away.

'Let go,' Kim said through her teeth.

'No chance,' replied Geena. She heaved on the magazine and it shot out of the bag like a cork out of a champagne bottle. Geena staggered backwards and dropped the magazine. Kim and Jazz immediately dived for it and banged their heads together.

'Oh dear,' I said, strolling over to the magazine and picking it up. 'Why didn't you just hand it over, Kim? It would have been a whole lot easier—'

I broke off. The whole front page of *Masala Express* was taken up with a huge photo of Molly

Mahal. She was glamorously dressed, and posing in what I recognized as Kim's living room. The headline read: BOLLYWOOD STAR TO TAKE PART IN OUR TOUCH THE CAR COMPETITION! READ ALL ABOUT IT ON PAGES FIVE AND SIX!

I shook the magazine at Kim. 'What's going on?'

'And how did you get this?' Geena grabbed the magazine from me. 'It's this week's edition. It's not even out yet.'

'From my neighbour,' Kim mumbled. 'The Chowdhurys' son, Miki. I told you, he works at the magazine.'

Jazz, who was still rubbing the side of her head, suddenly spotted the front cover. 'Molly Mahal in the Touch the Car competition?' she repeated incredulously. 'What's she doing *that* for?'

'Well, to get publicity for the school party,' Kim said eagerly. 'She talks about it in the interview.'

Geena flipped to pages five and six. There were more photos of Molly in different outfits (all Auntie's) and a short interview by Miki Chowdhury. It didn't tell us much we didn't already know. The only interesting bit was where Molly said she was currently staying with 'some very dear friends'. That made me smile. Or it would have done if she hadn't gone on to say that her future was looking a whole lot brighter than it had for the last few years, and she had quite a few irons in the fire. That sent a cold chill the length of my spine.

'Dad's one of her irons,' whispered Jazz in a doom-laden tone.

'So,' I said crossly to Kim, 'she came round to your place so that Miki Chowdhury could interview her, and now she's in the Touch the Car competition this weekend?'

'How very convenient,' remarked Geena. 'I'm sure *that* wasn't fixed at all.'

'Oh no,' Kim said earnestly. 'Her name was picked out of a hat. It was all fair and above board. She saw the competition in the copy of *Masala Express* that your paperboy gave her, and she entered it.'

'Leo!' I muttered. This was like a conspiracy. It *was* a conspiracy.

'I don't know why you're being so negative,' said Kim, looking puzzled. 'She's doing it for the school. You should be pleased. Think positive.'

'Why don't you just—?' I began with vigour, but Kim had already scuttled off.

'Dad's going to be very impressed if she wins,' Jazz predicted, like some tragic prophetess. 'She'll probably give him the car as a present.'

Geena and I jumped on her. It relieved our tension somewhat, but didn't solve the problem at all.

*

'She's doing *what*?' Auntie's eyebrows almost flew off the top of her head. 'What in God's name is a Touch the Car competition?'

'It's pretty self-explanatory,' I replied, handing her Kim's copy of *Masala Express*. After school, Kim had asked me to give it back in a reasonably assertive tone, but I had refused. Rather aggressively, I'm sorry to say.

Auntie scanned the article. 'Well!' she said at last. 'This beats everything, even for *her*.'

The front door opened. Molly and Dad came into the hall, laughing and chatting.

'Oh, hello, I saw Molly on the Broadway on my way home from work and gave her a lift,' Dad said defensively, all on one breath.

Molly had already spotted the copy of *Masala Express* in Auntie's hand. 'Oh, so you've found out my little secret,' she trilled with a smile that didn't quite reach her eyes. 'What do you think?'

Dad looked confused. 'What little secret?'

Silently Auntie handed him the magazine, and we all watched him closely for his reaction.

'Well!' said Dad at last. 'I think that's fantastic. And you're doing it for the school?'

'Oh, absolutely,' Molly agreed. 'The publicity will be excellent.'

Maybe I was being too sensitive. Or maybe I was just getting to know her a little better. Either way, there was something in her manner that didn't quite ring true.

'Are you going to sell the car and give the money to the school if you win?' I asked bluntly.

Molly smiled. 'Oh, I'm not going to win!' she said. 'Little old me up against two big strong men? I don't stand a chance.'

'She could take them on with one hand tied behind her back,' Jazz muttered sourly, as Molly swanned into the living room. 'And trample all over them.'

But was our dad the prize she was *really* going for?

The party was in less than two weeks, and after the party there was no reason for Molly Mahal to stay here any longer.

But by then it might be too late.

CHAPTER 10

The Touch the Car contest began on Friday afternoon at 5 p.m. By this time, it appeared that everyone in the school knew about it. It had become the single, the only topic of conversation at every opportunity – break time, lunch time and even during lessons. Mr Arora, like Dad, was almost overcome with admiration and, in our very hearing, had called Molly an 'inspirational woman'. Mr Grimwade was walking around in a daze, probably calculating how much money the school could raise if Molly sold the car and donated the profits. Molly Mahal T-shirts were everywhere like a rash. More posters had appeared along the Broadway. Tickets for the party were selling fast.

'What *are* Molly's chances of winning this ridiculous contest?' Geena asked. We were on our way to Mr Gill's Kwality Kar Emporium, where the competition was being held. Naturally, we weren't going to miss it.

'Oh, who knows?' I said. 'Standing and touching a car for hours doesn't seem to require a great deal of skill. Anyone could do it.'

'Ooh, no,' Jazz broke in. 'It's the ultimate endurance test. A battle of wills. You need mental toughness and physical stamina to succeed.'

Geena and I raised our eyebrows at her.

'I saw it on a website,' Jazz muttered.

'Do you want her to win?' I asked.

'Does it matter?' sighed Geena. 'If she wins, she'll impress everyone, including Dad. And if she loses, she'll be brave little Molly who did her best.'

'Where are these people *going*?' Jazz asked, perplexed, as a steady stream of students barged their way past us, all heading in the same direction. One of them was George Botley.

'George' – I tapped him on the shoulder – 'you live in the opposite direction, remember?'

'Ha ha, you're funny,' George retorted. 'I'm going to watch the Touch the Car competition.' He elbowed his way past us.

Geena cast up her eyes. 'We should have guessed,' she murmured.

'I hope we can get into the showroom,' said Jazz. 'I don't want to miss it.'

'Let's run,' I suggested.

We rushed off towards the Broadway, where the Kwality Kar Emporium was situated. However, the other people who were going that way soon got the idea, and eventually there was a big crowd of us all dashing down the Broadway like marathon runners. It did at least have the advantage of sweeping everybody else out of our path like a giant broom.

Mr Gill's emporium was already almost full, and at least half the people there were wearing Molly T-shirts. The showroom had been cleared of all the cars except for the prize of a silver Ford Ka, which stood on a raised platform in the middle of the floor, decorated with red ribbons. There was no sign of Molly yet.

'There's Mr Arora,' said Jazz as we pushed our way through the tall glass doors. Mr Gill, a short tubby figure dressed, strangely, in an ill-fitting dinner jacket and bow tie, was ushering people inside. 'And Mr Grimwade.'

'I do believe that's Leo next to him,' remarked Geena innocently.

I scowled. My face soured even more when I spotted Kim just behind Leo. She was chatting to a young Indian man in his twenties, wearing a baseball cap and baggy jeans and carrying a notebook and pen. I guessed that he was the Chowdhury neighbour who worked at *Masala Express*.

'Hello, girls.' We turned to see Uncle Dave

beaming at us. Behind him were Auntie Rita and Biji. 'Well, what do you think? Is Molly going to win the car?'

'She's quite old to stand for hours on end,' Auntie Rita sniped. 'Her back will probably give out.'

'It's ridiculous,' Biji grumbled. 'Touching a car? What kind of a foolish activity is that? Hey!' She waved her stick at Mr Gill. 'Don't you have a seat for a poor, helpless old lady?'

'About as helpless as a killer shark,' Jazz muttered, as Mr Gill rushed over with a plastic chair.

The showroom doors had been closed now, leaving a small crowd of people outside in the yard, their annoyed faces pressed against the glass. Among them I could see Mrs Dhaliwal and her entire family, and Mr Attwal.

The air of excitement in the showroom was almost tangible. There was a rustle of excitement as the office door opened, followed by a sigh of disappointment as Dad, Auntie and Mrs Macey stepped out. We edged our way through the crowd towards them.

'Where's Molly?' I asked.

Auntie raised her eyes heavenwards. 'All the contestants are in the office,' she said. 'Of course, Molly had to ask for a separate dressing room to "prepare" herself. Typical.'

'She needed somewhere private.' Dad leaped in to defend his heroine.

'Did she get her own room, then?' Geena asked.

'Well, they cleared out the cleaner's broom cupboard for her,' Auntie replied. 'When we left, she was demanding Perrier water and ginger biscuits. Once a diva, always a diva.' Her eyes strayed across the room towards Mr Arora, who was chatting to Mr Grimwade. Mr Arora glanced in our direction, and Auntie instantly withdrew her gaze.

'I'm sure Molly's going to win,' Mrs Macey said eagerly, looking as if this was the most exciting thing that had happened to her for years.

'Amber' – Kim had appeared from nowhere and was tugging at my arm – 'this is Miki, from *Masala Express*. He wants to ask you some questions about Molly.'

'All right?' the young man in the baseball cap said laconically. He flipped open a notebook. 'So you're friends of Molly Mahal's?'

'No, definitely not,' said Jazz.

'Yes, we are,' I said, stepping hard on her toes.

'Ouch,' Jazz grumbled.

I could see Miki Chowdhury's nostrils flaring as he scented the glimmer of a story.

'So how do you know her then?' he asked, becoming slightly more animated.

'We just do,' Geena said repressively.

'What's it like having a film star staying with you?' Miki queried.

'It's one long laugh from morning to evening,' I said.

Miki tapped his pen against his teeth. 'Any funny stories? Amusing anecdotes? Heart-warming happenings?'

'Not a single one,' I replied.

Miki shrugged. 'Thanks, you've been a great help,' he said in a heavily sarcastic tone before walking off.

Kim was looking disappointed. 'You could have been a bit more forthcoming,' she muttered.

'And told him what we *really* think of her?' I enquired. That sent her packing.

There was another rustle of anticipation as Mr Gill stepped up to the microphone, which had been placed at the side of the Ford Ka. The contest was about to start.

'Welcome,' began Mr Gill loudly. The microphone screeched and everyone covered their ears. It took a few minutes to adjust it, and then Mr Gill began again.

'We are gathered here today,' he said, with great pomp, 'to witness the ultimate endurance test. A battle of wills. A show of mental toughness and physical stamina . . .'

'He's seen the website,' Jazz whispered in my ear.

'We have three contestants here today who are going to strive to do their very, very best,' Mr Gill went on. 'And here at my Kwality Kar emporium, we also strive to give you the very, very best. For example, we have a Honda Civic, a very nice family car, going cheap for just—'

He was elbowed out of the way by Miki Chowdhury.

'Good afternoon, everyone,' he said. 'Please welcome the editor of *Masala Express*, Mrs Anjali Desai.'

There was a very faint smattering of applause, but people were also muttering with dissatisfaction. It was one minute to five o'clock and everyone was longing for the contest to start.

'May I say . . .' began Anjali Desai, who was all teeth and big hair and shiny gold jewellery. 'May I say how honoured I am to be here for today's competition. *Masala Express* has a very important place in the Asian community, and—'

'Get on with it,' called a voice which sounded suspiciously like George Botley's.

Mrs Desai drilled a contemptuous stare into the crowd. 'Our contestants in today's Touch the Car competition are Mr Vijay Anand, Mr Akbar Khan' – a few people clapped – 'and Miss Molly Mahal, the well-known Bollywood legend.'

The cheer that rang out almost lifted the roof off the showroom.

'No bias there at all then,' Geena muttered.

On cue, the office door opened. 'We Are the Champions' by Queen boomed out of the speakers, and we all pushed forward to get a better look. It was rather an anticlimax when two men trotted out. The first was short and plumply rounded and shoehorned into a shiny blue tracksuit. The second was tall and thin, hunched over like a mournful heron in shorts and singlet. There was no sign of Molly Mahal.

Mr Anand and Mr Khan advanced to the platform.

'Mr Anand?' Anjali Desai pulled the short, tubby man over to the microphone. 'What are your battle tactics?'

'I plan to keep myself going with high-energy snacks and plenty of water during our breaks,' puffed Mr Anand, who seemed breathless after just the short walk from office to platform. 'I'm going to win this contest!' He raised a clenched fist, and there was a faint cheer from some of his supporters in the crowd.

'And Mr Khan?' Mrs Desai turned to the mournful heron. 'How about you?'

Poor Mr Khan. Nobody heard a word he said.

For that was the moment Molly Mahal chose to make her entrance.

The office door opened again. Molly stepped out, and a hush descended on the whole audience. No tracksuits or shorts for her, but a gold sari, shimmering with deep purple embroidery, and high-heeled gold sandals. Her hair was swept up on top of her head and woven with purple blossoms. I could not have come up with a less suitable outfit for a Touch the Car competition if I'd thought about it for a week.

'That's not one of my saris,' Auntie said faintly. 'Where did she get it?'

'Those shoes,' breathed Geena. 'She won't be able to stand for five minutes.'

Seeming confident and relaxed, Molly Mahal walked through the audience towards the platform. She held her head high. Everyone was spellbound. The glossy sheen of celebrity was working its magic on everyone.

The clapping began. A wave of thunderous applause that reached its crescendo as Molly Mahal stepped onto the stage. There was absolutely no doubt who most of the audience wanted to win.

'Miss Mahal, welcome!' fussed Mrs Desai, taking her arm. Mr Khan, who had been rudely shoved aside, looked rather irate. 'How do you intend to approach this contest? Tell us something of your tactics.'

'My tactics?' Molly repeated huskily. You could have heard a pin drop in the showroom. 'My tactics are simple. I just want to do my best, even if I don't manage to win.'

There was another rousing cheer, although Mr Grimwade looked a bit concerned. Molly inclined her head graciously at the crowd and waved. Her fans went wild.

'Now, the rules,' announced Mrs Desai. 'The winner will be the person who remains standing and touching the car for the longest time. Contestants will be disqualified if they remove their hand from the car or if they fall asleep. There will be breaks of fifteen minutes every two hours, and twenty-five minutes every six hours.' She looked sternly at the contestants. 'Contestants will also be disqualified if they overrun their breaks. A representative from *Masala Express* will constantly be on duty, and their decision is final. Is that clear? Then let the contest begin.'

There was a rustle of anticipation as the three contestants took their places around the Ford Ka.

'Ready!' shouted Mrs Desai. 'Three . . . two . . . one. Hands on the car!'

There was a collective intake of breath as Molly Mahal, Mr Anand and Mr Khan placed their palms against the Ka's shiny silver surface. This was followed by loud applause. For ten minutes there was dead silence as we watched them with eager faces. Then people started coughing, shuffling their feet and whispering to each other.

What everyone had failed to realize was that watching three people standing touching a car is actually infinitely *boring*.

'It'll be more interesting when they get tired,' Geena assured us after twenty minutes. 'They'll start lurching around and hallucinating and falling asleep.'

'So will I, if I have to watch any more of this,' Jazz complained. 'I'm hungry.'

'We can't go yet,' said Dad. 'We have to stay and give Molly a bit of support.'

Mr Anand was already looking fidgety. He kept rocking backwards and forwards on the balls of his feet, and staring at the clock on the wall every minute. Mr Khan was hunched over even more, sighing loudly at short intervals. Only Molly stood still, her back straight, her head up, poised and still.

Over the next hour or so, people began to drift away, looking rather apologetic. By the time the second hour came round, half of the people in the showroom had left, and Jazz was whining like a five-year-old.

'Can't we go now? I'm *hungry*.'

Auntie tapped Dad's arm. 'I think we should go home and eat, Johnny.'

'You take the girls,' Dad said absently, his eyes fixed on Molly. 'I'll stay a bit longer.'

We slipped quietly over to the door. Molly must have seen us leaving, but didn't betray it by so much as a flicker of an eyelash. Not even when I gave her a little wave.

'That was rather stupid, wasn't it?' said Geena. 'What if she'd taken her hand off the car to wave back at you?'

That hadn't occurred to me, I must say. 'I imagine Mr Grimwade would have throttled me,' I replied.

Mr Grimwade and Mr Arora were still there, tucking into boxes of Kentucky Fried Chicken. Kim was with Miki Chowdhury, but Leo had gone, probably to do his paper deliveries. I couldn't see George Botley either.

We made our way to Auntie's car.

'Do you think Molly will win?' asked Jazz.

'Not in those shoes,' Auntie replied.

'It'll probably be all over by tomorrow morning,' Geena said wisely.

She was wrong, however. During the evening we watched TV while receiving regular calls and text messages from Dad. Nothing much seemed to be happening. At one point there was a minor bit of excitement when it was thought Mr Anand had given up and gone home. But it turned out that the smell of the KFC boxes had been too much for him and he'd popped out in his break to buy one.

Dad still wasn't back when we went to bed. Of course, Jazz thought this was of great significance.

'He won't desert Molly in her hour of need,' she said. 'He'll probably stay there all night.'

'That's ridiculous,' I said sharply. 'Of course he won't.'

But the idea must have got right inside my head, because I slept very badly. Dreams of Dad and Molly Mahal entwined with periods of wakefulness and fighting Jazz for the duvet. We both woke up heavy-eyed and bickering on Saturday morning, wondering what was going on at the Kwality Kar Emporium. We argued our way down the stairs to the kitchen, where Auntie was sitting with a cup of tea.

'Anything happen?' I demanded, without so much as a good morning.

Auntie shrugged. 'No. Apart from the fact that your dad stayed there all night.'

'Ha!' said Jazz triumphantly.

'We'd better take him some breakfast.' Auntie rose and took two flasks from the cupboard. 'Go and get dressed. Oh, and kick Geena out of bed.'

I raised my eyebrows. '*Two* flasks?'

Auntie looked uncomfortable. 'Well, I suppose Molly could do with a cup of tea herself.'

'You know,' said Jazz, 'you're quite nice, really.'

'Thank you,' Auntie replied, trying not to look pleased.

We levered Geena out of bed and were ready to leave in about half an hour. I was curious to find out how many people would still be at the Kwality Kar Emporium. The answer was, not many. Mrs Macey and Kim had gone, so had Anjali Desai. Mr Grimwade and Mr Arora were still there, though. They were sitting in the corner fast asleep, with their heads on each other's shoulders. Mr Grimwade's snores could be heard halfway down the Broadway. Mr Gill, the owner, was slumped on one of the sofas, yawning widely. Dad was next to him. Apart from that, there were only a very few other people there, all looking baggy-eyed and yawning non-stop.

There was also no sign of Molly Mahal or the other contestants.

'Is it all over, Dad?' I asked. 'Who won?'

Dad shook his head. 'No, they're having a break.' He yawned. 'I don't know how Molly's coping. She must be exhausted.'

'We've brought you some tea.' Auntie handed him one of the flasks.

'I'll take the other one to Molly,' I volunteered. I was secretly very curious to see how she was holding up.

'She's in her room,' Dad said with another almighty yawn. He seemed too weak to unscrew the flask and handed it back for Auntie to open, like a child. 'Miki Chowdhury wanted to talk to her.'

I took the carrier bag from Auntie. I thought someone from *Masala Express* might stop me going backstage, as it were, but nobody took any notice. I passed through the door and into a wide corridor. There were washrooms and the main office. The door was open. Mr Anand was flat out on the sofa breathing heavily, while Mr Khan was standing on his head chanting some mystic prayer. Neither of them looked like they were going to last another five minutes.

Further down the corridor I could hear the murmur of voices. I followed the sound.

I wished I hadn't. I simply wasn't expecting to hear what I heard next.

CHAPTER 11

When Miki Chowdhury finally came out of the room, I ducked out of sight round the corner. I waited until I heard his footsteps fade away down the corridor. Then I pushed open the door. Molly had been directing this movie for far too long. It was time someone else had a turn.

The room wasn't really much more than a big cupboard. But someone had tried to make it more comfortable by squeezing in an armchair and a tiny coffee table. Molly was crouched in the armchair, her bare feet resting on the table. Her toes were swollen and red. There were dark circles under her eyes.

'I've brought you some tea,' I said coldly. I was still reeling in shock from the conversation I'd listened to. 'Or maybe you'd like some champagne to celebrate. Oh. I forgot,' I went on sarcastically. 'You haven't won. Yet.'

Molly didn't look guilty at all. 'Do you often

sneak around listening to other people's conversations?' she enquired.

'Is that worse than cheating?' I asked. 'You tell me.'

Silence.

'Amber,' Molly began softly, 'you don't know what you're talking about.'

'Oh, but I do,' I said. '*Masala Express* want you to win the competition, and they're going to fix it so you do.'

It will be easy tonight. There'll be hardly anyone here. We can disqualify the other two for overrunning their breaks. No one will know, and they'll be too tired to care . . .

Miki Chowdhury's whispered words were still running through my head.

Molly sighed. 'No, Amber, you don't understand,' she said. 'I don't mean the contest. Publicity. Press. Media. How it works.'

'I don't want to.' My voice shook a little. 'It stinks.'

'It's a game,' Molly went on, ignoring me and speaking half to herself. She seemed too tired to care about putting on an act any more. 'It's all a game. Who do you think cares if Mr Anand or Mr Khan wins that car? No one. But if *I* win' – she turned the full force of her cat-like eyes on me – 'then it's a news story. It'll be everywhere. All over the Indian press and TV. Here and in India. *Masala Express* get great publicity and so—' She stopped herself, then continued, 'So does the school. Everybody's happy. Don't you see?'

'But it's not *fair*,' I said. Even to my own ears, I sounded like a five-year-old.

'This is how it works, Amber,' Molly replied wearily, rubbing her eyes. 'Don't tell me you never read gossip about celebrities in your glossy magazines? Half of it isn't true, do you realize that?'

'Of course I do,' I mumbled. I wasn't stupid.

Molly was barely listening. 'Some of it is planted by their PR people. Some of it is made up by the press. We feed them, and they feed on us. Like I said, it's a game. Sometimes you win, sometimes you lose.' Her face shadowed briefly. 'Like I said to you before, there's always a price to pay.'

I couldn't speak. I could – just – understand what she meant. But it felt wrong.

'Molly.' Dad put his head round the door. 'Your break's nearly over.'

He withdrew. Molly lowered her feet from the table and wiggled her toes.

'So you're really going to do it?' I asked. 'You're going to cheat?'

'It's called giving everyone what they want,' replied Molly.

'Well, I think you're wrong,' I said shakily. 'I

can't believe you'd do that. Not when all those people out there think you're so wonderful.'

I walked out. I was trembling. It was almost the longest conversation we'd ever had, and it had made me feel wretched.

'Amber?' Auntie studied me closely as I returned to the showroom. 'What's wrong?'

'I'm all right,' I said. 'Just a bit tired.'

'How's Molly?' asked Geena.

'Oh, she's just fine,' I said grimly.

The showroom was filling up again. There were all the usual suspects. Kim, Mrs Macey, George Botley, Mrs Dhaliwal, Mr Attwal and Leo. Mr Grimwade and Mr Arora had woken up and were yawning and stretching. They both looked embarrassed at being caught in such a cosy huddle.

There also seemed to be more reporters than yesterday, all clustered round Miki Chowdhury. There were several men and women clutching notebooks, and in one corner were a couple of men with TV cameras balanced on their shoulders.

'One's filming for an Indian TV station,' said Kim, who had edged her way over to me. 'And one's from the local news. Miki thinks someone from a national newspaper might come too!' She looked excited. 'And there are reporters from other Indian newspapers and magazines. Miki says it's great publicity for *Masala Express*, as well as the school.'

'Really,' I said coldly. 'And what else does Miki say?'

Kim looked puzzled. 'What do you mean?'

'Nothing.' I stopped myself from saying more. What was happening was wrong. But telling someone didn't seem the right thing to do either. Besides, who would believe me? I'd probably get lynched by a mad mob of Molly Mahal fans.

'Something's going on,' Geena said, as Kim left us. 'What is it, Amber?'

Jazz was hovering around too, looking curious.

'Nothing at all,' I said brightly.

'Oh, you're far too upbeat.' Geena stared closely at me. 'Is it something to do with Molly?'

I was saved from answering by the entrance of all three contestants, to thunderous applause and whoops. Molly looked calm and relaxed. I tried to catch her eye, but she stared straight ahead and wouldn't look at me as she took her place on the platform again. I did notice that she'd left the gold sandals behind and was wearing her trainers. I didn't realize the significance of this until later.

The contest began again. By now the showroom was packed to bursting. There were people crammed into the yard too, steaming up the windows as they pressed their faces against the glass. Because it was Saturday, people were shopping on the Broadway, and kept popping in to see what was going on. It added enormously to the crowd.

10.20 a.m. The air-conditioning failed. Everyone began to melt. It took a few frantic phone calls by Mr Gill to get it fixed, but it was boiling hot for over two hours. Mr Anand must have sweated off half his body weight by then. Dr Patel, from the surgery across the road, was on stand-by.

11.35 a.m. Mr Arora sneaked off home, looking as wrung out as a wet dishcloth. For a moment I thought he was going to come over and speak to us before he left, but he didn't. Mr Grimwade remained behind, looking dishevelled and with the beginnings of a scary beard.

1.15 p.m. George Botley shambled over to us and asked me if I wanted to go to McDonald's with him. I sent him away with a flea in his ear.

By this time the contest had been going on for about twenty hours. Almost a whole day. The strain was beginning to show. Mr Anand was perspiring heavily, pulling a handkerchief out of his pocket every few minutes to wipe his streaming face. Mr Khan didn't look much better. Molly was holding up well. But then she knew when the contest was going to end, didn't she? She only had to wait until the evening.

'Johnny, let's go home,' Auntie said at two o'clock. 'You're exhausted. And we must eat.'

'All right,' Dad said, following up with a jaw-cracking yawn. 'I can come back later.'

'Can I come with you?' I asked. 'And stay all night, I mean.' If Molly Mahal was going to cheat, I would take on the role of her conscience, I decided. I was going to be here to watch her do it. It wouldn't make any difference to her, but it might ease my own feelings of guilt.

'Now, why would you want to do that?' Geena said thoughtfully, as we pushed through the crowd.

'No reason,' I replied. Jazz poked me violently in the back. 'Ouch. Don't do that, please.'

'Tell us then,' she demanded.

'There's nothing to tell,' I replied.

Oh, how I wished that were true.

The first glimmer of excitement happened that night at just before 1 a.m. We had returned to the showroom a couple of hours earlier. At first, only Dad and I were going. Then Geena, determined to find out what was going on, said she'd come too. Jazz didn't want to be left out, but brought her sleeping bag. Auntie decided that if everyone else was going, she might as well come along for the ride.

There had still been quite a few people earlier, but now, after midnight, there was almost no one.

Even Mr Grimwade had staggered out an hour or so before. The only person left who I knew was Miki Chowdhury, and I eyed him with dislike.

The three contestants were now looking exhausted and stressed after almost thirty-two hours. Mr Anand was lurching about and muttering to himself, only just managing to keep in contact with the car. Mr Khan kept standing on one foot to relieve tired legs, which made him look even more like a heron. Molly was trying to remain upright, but was swaying slightly and kept closing her eyes.

I wondered when Miki Chowdhury planned to get the other two disqualified.

Then, suddenly, Mr Anand stumbled forward, swaying dizzily. Just for a second, his hand came off the car and flapped about in the air.

'That's it!' Miki Chowdhury shouted triumphantly, jumping forward. 'Mr Anand, you're out!'

There were a few weak protests from a couple of people, who must have been Mr Anand's relatives. Miki took no notice and waved them aside. Looking disgruntled, the family moved in and bore a dazed Mr Anand away.

'Did I miss something?' Jazz, who had been rolled up in her sleeping bag in the corner, sat up.

'Yes,' replied Geena. 'Mr Anand's a goner.'

'Oh, really!' Jazz said crossly. 'I was only having

a little nap. Couldn't he have hung on for five more measly minutes?'

'It seems not,' I said. 'It was very inconsiderate of him.'

Neither Molly nor Mr Khan showed any reaction to Mr Anand keeling over. Mr Khan was too busy muttering to himself, and Molly had her eyes closed again. I checked my watch. It was time for a fifteen-minute break. At Miki's signal, Molly and Mr Khan stumbled over to the door and disappeared.

My throat tightened up. I wondered what would happen.

'Amber, you're as jumpy as a nest full of ants,' remarked Geena as we waited for them to return. 'Are you going to tell us what's going on, or must we use force?'

I did not reply. When the office door opened, I was watching. My insides were twisted and tied up in intricate knots. I felt sick.

Molly Mahal came out, followed by Mr Khan. Both of them resumed their places at the car.

The same thing happened after the 3 a.m. break. By this time my eyes were red and gritty and sore. Geena had squashed into Jazz's sleeping bag with her. Both of them were asleep. Dad was sitting on the floor with his back against the wall, his head on his knees. Auntie had found a secretary's chair and was perched on it, fast asleep, rotating gently round and round. I was the only one who was awake. I was sick with exhaustion and beginning to think that it was me who was hallucinating. But at last, as the time ticked round to the 5 a.m. break, it finally began to penetrate my dazed skull. Mr Khan was still in the contest. Miki Chowdhury was looking annoyed. There'd been no cheating. Molly wanted to win fair and square.

I wanted to believe that what I'd said had made a difference, but I thought it was much more likely that Molly was nervous I might tell somebody what I'd overheard. Like Dad, for instance. That would have ruined her great plan.

People started arriving again at about eight o'clock in the morning. This time the crush had to be seen to be believed. There were more newspaper reporters and four cameramen this time. Mrs Dhaliwal almost had a fight with one who got in her way. The showroom filled up in record time, and still there were people flooding in the gates and trying to push their way through the doors.

I looked round with bloodshot eyes. Kim was back, looking as fresh as a daisy; Mrs Macey was there, and Leo, hugging a huge bag of Sunday newspapers. Mr Grimwade and Mr Arora, shaved and washed, had returned too.

In the middle of all of them stood Molly and Mr

Khan. 'Stood' doesn't really describe it as they were both barely upright. Molly was talking to herself. She seemed to be repeating dialogue from her films. I could catch bits from *Amir Ladka, Garib Ladka*. Mr Khan was just groaning. They had been standing there now, with only short breaks, for forty hours.

At precisely 9.42 a.m. it finally happened. Mr Khan's legs began to collapse. His ankles seemed to go first. He wobbled. Then his legs concertinaed underneath him, and he collapsed in a huddled mass on the floor.

There was shocked silence for a moment. Then a huge cheer almost lifted off the roof. I glanced across at Miki Chowdhury and Anjali Desai. They both looked utterly delighted.

'Mr Khan is disqualified,' announced Mrs Desai, barely able to control a triumphant smirk. 'The winner of our Touch the Car competition is Bollywood legend, Miss Molly Mahal!'

Molly seemed too dazed to take in what was happening. She remained standing with her hand on the car until Miki Chowdhury and Mr Grimwade rushed over to escort her to a chair. A glass of water was handed to her.

I watched in silence as there was more tumultuous applause. At least she'd won it fairly. Maybe what I'd said had made a difference. I couldn't know. I was completely sure she'd never tell me.

Molly was struggling to her feet, indicating that she wanted to say something.

'Miss Mahal, congratulations on your fabulous victory,' proclaimed Mrs Desai. She thrust the microphone under Molly's nose. 'What do you plan to do with your prize?'

Mr Grimwade was pushing his way forward, his face alight with expectation. I glanced at Dad. He was beaming with delight.

'I will be selling the car,' said Molly faintly. 'And I plan to donate the money to a very good cause.'

Mr Grimwade looked thrilled.

'This young man is Leo Barnett.' Molly motioned to Leo to come towards her. He did so, looking puzzled. 'Leo has a brother who needs an operation very seriously. To have that operation, the family are saving to take him to America. I intend to sell the car and donate the money to the Barnett family.'

There was a loud gasp. Leo clapped his hand to his mouth, looking stunned. Then a roar of applause and approval and hands clapping as if they couldn't clap any harder. Flashbulbs popped and cameras rolled.

Molly Mahal had really excelled herself this time.

*

And so . . .

For the next week, Molly was everywhere. She made the local newspapers and the local TV news. The whole of the next issue of *Masala Express* was devoted to her. She even got a column or two in some of the national papers, and one had a small photo. Asha, Auntie's friend in Delhi, phoned to tell us that the contest had also been shown on Indian TV. The Indian press at home and back in India were all wild to interview her.

It seemed ridiculous. Becoming famous again simply for touching a car *was* ridiculous. But then celebrities were doing crazy things all over the place to get noticed. Living in jungles, being shipwrecked on desert islands or locked up in houses with each other for weeks. Touching a car didn't really seem so stupid, after all.

Molly was a local heroine. We hardly ever saw her. She spent hours on the phone, and couldn't leave our house without people asking for her autograph. She was offered free meals in restaurants, free clothes, shoes, jewellery, make-up. Leo's mum and dad invited her to visit, and there were more pictures of her in the local newspaper with Leo's brother Keith. Although Mr Grimwade was a bit peeved to miss out on the car, he couldn't complain about the publicity. The Bollywood party was completely sold out, and several local Indian businessmen had made big donations to the school fund after Molly had sweet-talked them into it.

Molly loved all the attention.

But she and I never discussed what had happened that night.

The day of the party came round. No lessons for us. We spent the whole day, along with the other volunteers, decorating the school hall for the evening's festivities. Auntie came along to supervise, and studiously avoided Mr Arora for the whole seven hours. He, in turn, strenuously avoided her too.

'Look at that pair,' Geena said. We watched Mr Arora take an elaborate route past baskets of flowers and heaps of tinsel and piles of rolled-up film posters, just so that he didn't have to walk past Auntie. 'Couldn't you just bang their heads together?'

'Wait till tonight,' I predicted. 'Molly will be the belle of the ball, and Auntie will be seriously displeased.'

'Well, she'd better get used to it,' Jazz muttered. 'Molly's everywhere like a rash at the moment.'

'Including all over Dad?' asked Geena gravely.

'That's something we have to sort out, straight after the party.' I looked from one to the other. 'I mean, like we said, there's no reason why she has to stay with us any longer then.'

'Oh, my,' said Geena. 'I can just see us chucking her out onto the streets with nowhere to go. That would be headline news in *Masala Express*.'

'INDIAN FAMILY IN HOSPITALITY SHOCKER – HEARTLESS DHILLONS EVICT HEROINE MOLLY,' Jazz speculated.

I groaned. The situation seemed to have become more complicated, not less.

Kim was sitting on the other side of the hall, concentrating on threading flowerheads onto string. I went up to her.

'What are you wearing tonight?' I asked.

Kim glanced up. 'Oh, just my jeans.'

'I brought a suit for you to borrow,' I told her. 'A pink one. I think it will fit you. There's a bindi to match.'

'Thanks, Amber.' Kim looked thrilled.

'That's all right.' I left her surrounded by flowers. We were still friends. It wasn't Kim's fault that she'd heard the siren call of Molly Mahal and become her devoted slave.

When it was finished, the hall was spectacular. Painted film posters were fixed to the walls; sequinned and embroidered red, gold and white saris swathed the windows; there were garlands of flowers, gold foil paper chains, shiny tinsel and tiny white fairy lights everywhere.

'It looks wonderful,' said Mr Grimwade, who

had appeared, magically, as the last decoration was pinned into place. 'Well done, all of you.'

Auntie was silent as we left to go home and change. She seemed tired and depressed. There wasn't a party atmosphere at all, not in our house at least. It didn't seem the right moment to bring up the question of what we were going to do about Molly after the party. Not then.

But nothing – *nothing* – could have prepared us for what happened when we arrived home.

'I'm hungry,' Jazz said, throwing her bag onto the coffee table. 'What's for tea?'

'Nothing,' Auntie replied unsympathetically. 'We'll be eating later at the party.'

I left them beginning what promised to be quite a bitter argument and slipped upstairs. I was going to sneak in and take the first shower to make sure I had plenty of hot water.

I never got to the bathroom. Molly's bedroom door stood wide, and I glanced in casually, as you do. I noticed that the battered suitcase, which had stood in the corner ever since she arrived, had gone.

Puzzled, I peered into the room. I opened the wardrobe. Auntie's clothes were still there, but Molly's weren't. I could not believe my eyes.

'She's gone!' I almost tripped over my own feet

as I dashed back down the stairs. I could hardly believe that our problem had been so simply and easily solved. 'Molly's left. She's moved out.'

'Who's gone?' asked Jazz stupidly.

Auntie and Geena stared at me.

'Molly,' I replied. 'Her suitcase's gone, and all her stuff.'

Jazz dashed out of the room and up the stairs as if she didn't quite believe me and wanted to see for herself. Auntie sat down rather heavily on the sofa as if her legs had suddenly collapsed beneath her.

'She's really gone?' Geena exclaimed. 'And she didn't leave a note or anything?'

'It doesn't look like it,' I replied, suddenly feeling a little hurt. But why should I expect anything more where Molly Mahal was concerned?

I remembered when Auntie had left us so abruptly, just a month or two ago, to return to India. We'd gone after her and brought her back. We wouldn't be going after Molly Mahal.

'Oh my God,' Auntie groaned. 'What about the party?'

Geena let out a shriek, and I put my hands to my face. The horror. We had five hundred guests who had paid to see a Bollywood film star, and now we didn't have a clue where that film star was.

We heard Jazz clattering down the stairs again. Her face was a picture. 'Dad's gone with her,' she said tragically. 'They must have eloped.'

CHAPTER 12

'WHAT!' Auntie screamed.

'Don't be ridiculous,' I snapped.

'Jazz, this is no time to play the drama queen,' Geena pointed out irritably. 'Be quiet.'

'His best suit's gone,' Jazz said in a small voice. 'And his posh shirt and tie. *And* his shaving stuff.'

My knees wobbled under me and I clutched at Geena for support.

'Are you sure?' Auntie demanded.

Jazz nodded, her bottom lip trembling.

Auntie muttered something under her breath which might have been a prayer, and dived for the phone. She punched in Dad's mobile number, and we all waited.

'I can't get through,' she said, banging the receiver down. She then tried his direct line at work. This time, an answerphone message. Dad wouldn't be in the office again that day.

We stood there looking at each other as if we were completely paralysed. I couldn't begin to untangle the heaving mass of emotions inside me.

'Dad wouldn't do something like this,' said Geena at last. But it wasn't convincing.

'They must have decided to get married and tell us later,' Jazz said, her eyes huge. 'You know, a fat accomplice.'

'A *fait accompli*,' I said absently. For once, I did not have a single idea in my head. Not a one. I looked appealingly at Auntie. And I can honestly say, for almost the first time since she moved in, that I was just so glad she was there.

'I'm sure there's a simple explanation.' Auntie visibly pulled herself together. 'Did any of you see him this morning?'

We shook our heads.

'He was in the bathroom when we left,' said Geena. 'We went early because of the party.'

'He seemed all right last night,' I added. He didn't seem like a man who was planning to run away and get married the following day.

'Geena, get your mobile and send your dad a text message,' Auntie ordered. 'We can't do anything until we find out where he is, but we'll have to let the school know that it's very unlikely Molly will be at the party tonight.'

I felt faint at the thought of five hundred guests turning up, and no Molly.

'Maybe he and Molly will arrive at the party and announce that they've got married,' suggested Jazz, looking rather sick.

'So why has Molly taken all her stuff with her then?' I demanded.

We stared blankly at each other. There didn't seem to be a suitable explanation to cover all the options.

Looking grim, Auntie dialled the school's number. 'No one's answering,' she said in frustration.

'Everyone's probably gone home early to get ready for the party,' I said. 'We could try Mr Grimwade or Mr Arora at home.'

'Except we don't have their numbers,' Jazz pointed out.

Auntie cleared her throat. 'Actually, I have Jai Arora's number,' she said in a too-casual voice. 'He gave it to me when we decided to organize the party together.'

Even Jazz was too worried about Dad to make any sort of knowing comment. We waited as Auntie tapped in the number. To our relief, it was answered almost straight away.

'Hello? May I speak to Mr Arora, please?' Auntie frowned, then slipped seamlessly from English into Punjabi. 'My name? Surinder Dhillon.' There was a pause. 'I'm just a friend. Well, my nieces go to the school where he teaches. No, I'm not married.'

Jazz and I raised our eyebrows at each other.

'That's not why I'm phoning at all.' Auntie's voice had an irritated edge. 'Is he there? It's very important.' We could hear an excited stream of Punjabi at the other end of the line. 'Well, thank you. Goodbye.'

'Who was that?' I asked, as Auntie slammed the phone down really rather hard.

'Some elderly female relative, by the sound of it,' Auntie said crossly. 'She practically accused me of stalking him!' She restrained herself with an effort. 'He's not there, anyway.'

'What do we do now then?' asked Jazz.

Auntie glanced at her watch. 'We'll have to go to the school now, and wait for Mr Grimwade or Mr Arora to turn up,' she said. 'We were going early anyway to organize the food. You'd better go and get changed, girls.'

'What about Dad?' I asked with dread.

'He's still not replying,' said Geena, hunched on the sofa with her phone clutched in her hand.

Auntie sighed. 'Appalling as it may sound, there's nothing we can do,' she said, 'except wait and see. But we might just about manage to save the party.'

'I don't feel like going to a party,' Jazz said

quietly as we trailed up the stairs, one after the other. 'It feels more like a funeral.'

'Yes,' said Geena. 'Ours.'

I had never felt less like getting dressed up. I'd already decided what I was going to wear – an orange tie-dyed suit with gold jewellery. It meant I could throw the outfit on without thinking about it.

'Will you call Molly Mum?' asked Jazz, not caring that her bindi was crooked.

'Don't be an idiot,' I retorted, and that was the extent of our conversation while we were changing.

The drive to school was grim and upsetting. Auntie tried not to speed, but some of her cornering had us clutching each other for safety. There wasn't any point anyway. When we reached the school, the only people who were around were the caretaker, some of the canteen staff, who'd been hired for the evening to lay the food out, and Chapati MC, who was assembling his decks on the stage.

Auntie began directing operations while we retired to a corner of the hall and sat on the floor, staring at Geena's phone and listening for the comforting *beep beep* that would tell us she had a new text message. It never came.

'I can't believe Dad would do this,' I said despondently.

'You just don't want to believe it,' Jazz butted in. 'I've been warning you for days.'

'We don't know anything yet,' Geena said sharply. 'Will you two shut up!'

'Don't tell me to shut up,' Jazz said in a raised voice.

'Oh, bickering, the perfect solution to our problem,' remarked Geena pompously.

We began elbowing each other, and who can say where it would have ended if Mr Grimwade hadn't walked into the hall at that very moment.

'Ah, Miss Dhillon,' he said, beaming at the long trestle tables laden with food. 'Everything going smoothly?'

'Not at all,' said Auntie tensely. 'Molly Mahal has disappeared.'

Mr Grimwade's jowls began to shake. 'D-d-dis-appeared?'

'She's packed up her things and gone,' Auntie told him. 'We don't know where.'

'But . . .' Mr Grimwade was so despairing, he could hardly get the words out. 'There are people queuing outside already. What are we going to *do*?'

I scrambled to my feet and peered through the glass doors. The queue already had twenty people in it, and it was growing every second. There were cars lining up to get into the car park, even though it was only 7 p.m. and the doors didn't officially open till 7.30. Mrs Dhaliwal was at the front of the queue in a shockingly pink sari.

Mr Grimwade clapped a hand to his forehead. 'How are we going to tell them that Molly Mahal isn't coming after all?' he groaned.

It was very unfortunate that, at this moment, Mr Arora chose to push open the door and enter the hall.

'Molly Mahal's not coming?' he repeated in a shocked voice, pausing in the open doorway.

'MOLLY MAHAL'S NOT COMING?' roared Mrs Dhaliwal in horror. And the mantra was repeated right down to the back of the ever-increasing queue.

'Oh dear,' said Geena. 'Now this really does mean trouble.'

Things began to happen quickly. Mr Arora was shunted into the hall at speed by the crowd surging forward. Mrs Dhaliwal led the charge, and suddenly Mr Grimwade was surrounded by irate party-goers.

'Molly's not coming?' Mrs Dhaliwal said furiously. 'Have you been selling tickets under false pretences, Mr Grimble?'

'Grimwade. And no, of course, we haven't.' Mr Grimwade took out a hanky and mopped his sweating brow. 'It's just that – there's been a slight hitch—'

'What hitch?' called George Botley, sauntering in and smirking at the sight of his arch-enemy in big trouble.

More people were cramming their way through the doors. Mr Attwal, Leo and his family, his dad carrying Keith, and Mrs Macey.

'Please, can we see your tickets?' Mr Arora shouted, trying to take some control of the situation. But he was forced to step aside to avoid being trampled to bits.

There, at the back of the next rush of people, was Kim, looking pretty and very un-Kim-like in my pink suit. And then behind her . . .

Oh, thank you. *Thank you.*

'DAD!'

Geena, Jazz and I screamed the word aloud. No one heard – they were too busy harassing Mr Grimwade. We flew across the hall on winged feet of joy, and all three of us flung ourselves into Dad's arms.

'That's a nice welcome,' said Dad, looking slightly bemused. 'Did you think I wasn't coming?'

'We weren't sure,' I said, finding it hard to catch my breath. He looked so normal and ordinary and Dad-like, I knew everything was all right.

'Johnny!' Auntie appeared behind us and threw her arms round Dad's neck. 'It's so wonderful to see you.'

Now Dad looked really bewildered. 'Well, thank you.'

'Where've you been, Dad?' Geena asked, hanging onto his arm. 'We've been phoning and texting you.'

'I was in a meeting at one of our suppliers all afternoon, so I turned my phone off,' Dad replied. 'I knew I'd be late, so I took my suit to work and got ready there before I left for the meeting.'

'Oh, what a simple explanation,' Geena remarked, cuffing Jazz lightly round the ear.

'It was an easy conclusion to jump to,' Jazz grumbled.

'What's going on?' Dad asked, as the angry crowd finally caught his attention. 'Where's Molly?'

Auntie quickly explained, and we watched Dad closely. He looked disappointed to hear that Molly had left without a word, but more concerned that there was a possible riot developing. More people were arriving and joining in the shouting.

'Amber?' Kim hurried over, her face pale and concerned. 'Where's Molly?'

I shrugged. Into the maelstrom came Mrs Capstick, the school secretary, with a white envelope in her hand. She carved out a path to Mr Grimwade and handed the envelope to him.

'Silence!' shouted Mr Grimwade.

The noise died away to a dissatisfied muttering.

'Now, I can understand that you are all very upset,' Mr Grimwade blustered, 'but I have just been informed that Miss Mahal left a letter with the school secretary earlier today. Hopefully this will explain her absence tonight. Of course, if I'd been given it earlier . . .' He cast a look of daggers at Mrs Capstick.

'I've been run off my feet,' she muttered defensively. 'I forgot.'

There was not a sound in the hall as Mr Grimwade opened the envelope.

'*Dear friends,*' Mr Grimwade read, '*I am so sorry I cannot be with you tonight as promised. But I hope you will be pleased for me. You see, something wonderful has happened. I have been offered a role in a new Bollywood film. The actress who was taking the part has fallen ill, so I am required at very short notice, and must travel to India today. I will be playing the part of the hero's mother, rather than his girlfriend, as I did in the past, but I expect I will get used to having a son who is only ten years younger than I am.*

I hope you will forgive me, that you will enjoy your party and that you will also enjoy the enclosed gift.

With all good wishes,

Molly.'

Mr Grimwade drew something else out of the envelope. 'It's a cheque for the school,' he gasped, his eyes almost popping out of his head. 'For one thousand pounds!'

'Post-dated,' Auntie whispered as she glanced over Mr Grimwade's shoulder. 'She can't have been paid for the film yet.'

There was a spontaneous burst of applause. I smiled. So that was the close of the story, that was how the movie ended. Molly had got what she had probably wanted all along. She'd gone back to the world of Bollywood, the only one she'd ever really known. I hoped that this time she would be happy.

'But she's not here, is she?' said Mrs Dhaliwal rebelliously. 'And that's what we paid for.' Other people began to mutter in agreement.

'I'm sure the school will reimburse anyone who wishes to return their ticket and leave now,' Mr Arora cut in.

'Oh,' said Mr Grimwade weakly. 'Yes, of course.'

'We should be compensated, too,' grumbled a woman I recognized as Mrs Dhaliwal's sister-in-law.

'Stop it.'

The voice was raised. It was beside me. It was *Kim's*. I turned to stare at her, as did everyone else.

'We should be pleased for Molly.' Kim was as pink as Mrs Dhaliwal's sari, but managing to force the words out. 'It's about time she had something for herself. I mean, she helped the school and she helped Leo's brother—'

'Yes, she did,' Leo said firmly. 'I'm really happy for her, and I hope her film is a great big success.'

There was silence.

'They're right,' said Mr Arora. 'Molly did her best for us. We should all wish her well.' He glanced around the hall. 'Does anyone still want to leave?'

No one moved.

'Well, then,' said Mr Arora, with an enquiring glance at Auntie, who blushed delicately, 'I believe we *are* supposed to be having a party?'

And so we did. What a party it was. All right, I had to spend the first half hour reviving Kim with fruit juice after her astonishing display of assertiveness. But while I was sitting and fanning her with a paper napkin, I overheard Mr Arora talking to Auntie. Apologizing, actually.

'You've done a magnificent job, organizing all this.' Mr Arora cleared his throat and fiddled with his purple tie. 'I feel like – I – er – didn't help as much as I could have done.' He coughed. 'I was a little taken up with Molly. I'm sorry.'

'It's all right,' Auntie replied. 'If it wasn't for Molly, the party wouldn't have been such a huge success.' Which was pretty generous of her, considering.

Mr Arora was standing with his back to me, so, unseen, I leaned out and gave Auntie a thumbs-up. She wagged her finger at me, but I don't think she was annoyed. Rather the reverse. However, she did lead Mr Arora away then, so that I couldn't hear any more. A bit mean, don't you think?

The party couldn't have gone with more of a swing if we'd had a hundred Bollywood stars there. Chapati MC almost blasted the new roof off the hall. I danced with Dad, with Leo and, yes, even with George Botley. I danced with Mr Arora too, when I could get him away from Auntie. Things were looking very promising again there.

But the highlight of the evening was when Mr Grimwade attempted to dance with the bhangra group. A sight never to be forgotten, beating even his appearance at the school's *Grease* prom party in a black leather jacket the year before.

There were only two things which troubled me. I couldn't stop wondering whether Molly had been planning for something like this all along. If she'd been using us for her own reasons. After all, it was the Touch the Car competition that had brought her back to everyone's attention. And then I shrugged and repeated to myself what Kim had said. Everyone was happy. Did it really matter?

The other was that she hadn't left us a note to say thank you for having her. But there I was wrong. There *was* a note on the table in the living room, in the very spot where Jazz had flung her bag down earlier that evening. It was simple, short and to the point.

Dear Amber,
You and your family have been very kind to me for the last few weeks, and I appreciate it very much. The enclosed is for you, with my thanks.

Molly

Inside the envelope was Molly's slim gold bangle. I felt quite overwhelmed and almost tearful, just for a moment. It had been important to her, and she'd left it for me. That had to mean something.

'I've changed my mind,' Jazz said, as the three of us fought for a space in the bathroom late that night. 'I don't want to be famous, after all.'

'Oh, I get it,' said Geena gravely. 'You've seen the heartache behind the smiles for the camera, the tears behind the designer dresses and the limousines and the enormous houses.'

'No.' Jazz shook her head. 'It just seems like too much bother.'

Geena and I giggled.

'Oh, well,' said Geena, 'I expect the world will survive without Jazz Dhillon, superstar.'

'It's all right for Molly,' Jazz went on, her mouth foaming with toothpaste. 'She hasn't got any family.'

'What do you mean?' I asked.

'Well, can you imagine what would happen if I got famous?' Jazz pointed her toothbrush accusingly at me and Geena. 'You two would tell the newspapers every single embarrassing thing you could think of about me.'

'Oh,' said Geena. 'You mean like when Dad took us horse-riding, and you fell off and landed smack in a cowpat?'

'That was funny,' I agreed. 'But not as funny as the time she tried to blow out the candles on her birthday cake, overbalanced and ended up with a face-full of cream sponge.'

'See?' Jazz said self-righteously. 'That's *exactly* what I mean.'

'You're right.' I grinned at Geena, and then neatly slid a blob of toothpaste down the back of Jazz's pyjama jacket. 'You can't trust us one bit.'

And during the uproar that followed, I remember thinking that, if it was a choice between fame and family, I knew which one I'd choose.

Every time.

ABOUT THE AUTHOR

Narinder Dhami is one of three sisters – just like Amber, Geena and Jazz! Narinder originally worked as a primary school teacher but always loved writing. After winning a few writing competitions, she was encouraged to take the leap to work on a book full-time. *Bollywood Babes* is Narinder's fourth book for Corgi and she is busily working on a further sequel about the sisters – *Bhangra Babes* – due to be published in early 2005.

To relax, Narinder loves reading murder mysteries, watching football and she is learning Italian. Narinder lives in Cambridge with her husband and four cats. For loads more information, an exclusive web-story and lots of fun stuff, visit www.narinderdhami.com.

Check out Amber, Jazz and Geena's first appearance in print . . .

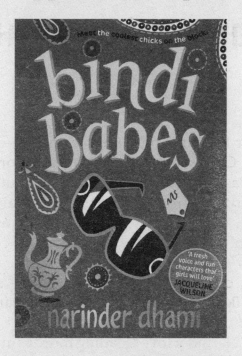

These girls have been through tough times, but now that they've got their perfect world sorted, the one fashion accessory they don't need is an interfering live-in auntie trying to cramp their style.

Bring on the collective power of the Bindi Babes! Nothing in life, not even their formidable Auntie-ji, can stop these sisters . . . can it?

'This refreshing madcap caper . . . is highly entertaining'
The Guardian

CORGI YEARLING BOOKS
ISBN 978 0 440 86512 4

Everyone agrees – Amber, Jazz and Geena are BABES!

The sisters have always been the most popular girls in the school – until now . . .

Suddenly there's a tough new girl who is resistant to the sisters' charm. And a gorgeous new guy who doesn't seem interested in any of them. Something's got to change . . . Taking a tip from their interfering auntie's book, the girls come up with a scheme to forge a friendship, get the guy and bounce right back . . .

'Fast paced . . . plenty of upbeat dialogue'
Irish Times

CORGI YEARLING BOOKS
ISBN 978 0 440 86628 2

I knew they were whispering behind my back . . .

Sunita has just started at Coppergate School but has to
be ultra-careful about making friends. She's scared someone
will discover her horrible secret. Unfortunately her worse
fears come true when she makes an enemy of Celina,
the class goddess . . .

With the secret out, Sunita has to prove that she's not like her
fraudster dad and tries to keep her head down. But she can't
hide her natural instinct for helping people and starts doing
little favours for people without them knowing.

Will more secrets mean more trouble for Sunita?

CORGI YEARLING BOOKS
ISBN 978 0 440 86629 9

The Bindi babes are back, and destined for stardom!

The Bindi Babes love a challenge! Amber, Jazz and Geena want to have the new school library named after their mum. They have a genius plan to raise funds for it – they're going to stage an amazing reality experiment. The sixth form block is turning into a Big Brother-style house for one week only – and they're going to be the stars. With spoilt relatives, film stars and love-struck boys in the mix, they know it's not going to be easy but the babes can handle it – can't they?

'A fresh voice and fun characters that girls will love'
Jacqueline Wilson

CORGI YEARLING BOOKS
ISBN 978 0 440 86729 6